DANCE TIME

DANCE TIME

A NOVEL BY
BEVERLY JABLONS

WILLIAM MORROW AND COMPANY, INC.
NEW YORK   1979

Grateful acknowledgment is made for permission to quote selected lyrics from the following songs:

"Manhattan" by Richard Rodgers and Lorenz Hart. Copyright © Edward B. Marks Music Corporation. Used by permission.

"You're My Everything" by Mort Dixon, Harry Warren, Joe Young. Copyright © 1931 Harms, Inc. Renewed 1959 Warock Corp. Used by permission.

Library of Congress Cataloging in Publication Data

Jablons, Beverly.
    Dance time.

    I. Title.
PZ4.J117Dan   [PS3560.A117]   813'.5'4   79-15755
ISBN 0-688-03517-5

Printed in the United States of America.

First Edition

1 2 3 4 5 6 7 8 9 10

FOR NICK,
JOSHUA AND ELISSA
... AND JOANNA

". . . men and women . . . they who are always bothering one another with all their self-importance and self-complacence, their self-pity, their feelings of inferiority and superiority; bothering one another more mysteriously with their dreams and needs, their formidable attractions and shinings, because of the hunger of each for the love of the other, and their actual need to be in each other's arms."

A Letter to St. Augustine
by HANIEL LONG

FRIDAY
NIGHT

1

The lock in the door to Ginny's apartment would not turn. The key slid in and then remained implacably rigid. Maryann forced it fiercely, willing it to turn in one direction or another. She pulled on the knob, hoping to shake loose some particle of dust, a mote, that might be causing it to jam. She took out her comb and tapped around the circular metal plate as though it were a jar of pickles. Perspiration beaded her upper lip and her flower-print blouse was a decoupage glued to her skin.

That was why Maryann was leaning against an apartment building on East Seventy-eighth Street in New York City on that particular Friday night in July, should anyone have asked. Some stranger or an old friend from Chagrin Falls or anybody at all.

The humid evening fog made her seem a vaporous uncertain figure and she stood quite still, as though the moment were uneventful. She didn't even notice the glossy, spindly-legged Italian greyhound that rushed out of the lobby of the building until, with an ecstatic quiver, he lifted his hind leg against Maryann's red-leather cosmetic case resting on the sidewalk next to her, even before the man holding the leash emerged through the door.

"Itsapoorbaby," the man cried from his own spindly frame, a medallion on a chain tumbling out of the dark bush on his chest as he leaned down to croon: "Itsapoorbaby, toodn't wait, m'baby toodn't wait."

The words emerged as a mantra lodged in his nose and he smiled fetchingly at Maryann, who refused to meet his eyes, share his love or grant penance. Instead, she unwaveringly watched the urine slide under the leather binding and make a long wet free-form gash on the pavement, like a mad Rorschach symbol.

A deep sigh became a shudder as she lifted the bag and took a few tentative steps to the right, barely avoiding drops of water that leaked from an air conditioner on the fourth floor. Maryann's hiccough was a sob.

"Go to New York and have a good time," said Jack Mansfield. That's how it all started. "It's time you did that kind of thing. See Ginny. You haven't seen her for a while. Maybe," he said, forcing a spoonful of butter almond ice cream into her resisting mouth (it was before dinner; he was consoling himself in anticipation of Maryann's objections, confusion, hurt), "maybe she's learned a few new words." Sweet Ginny, whose vocabulary had always been insufficient even at college, spoke in sighs and onomatopoeias.

Jack was going to a four-day seminar on insurance underwriting at the new conference center; the boys were at camp and she had rejected his other suggestions: visit her mother in Toledo; her brother in Phoenix; his mother at the cottage on the Upper Peninsula; his sister in the adjoining cottage. Then he grasped an image of Maryann's old college roommate living in New York and thought it was a brilliant idea. "Jack the Brilliant," he said, waving a spoon. "It's a great idea, Maryann." (Ever since her sons were born, the only time Maryann had traveled alone was to see her mother in Toledo.)

The interoffice memo, signed by the president of Jack's company, rested on the kitchen table between them, absorbing stains of ice-cream droppings. No wives, it said, no distractions. All the men protested vigorously and vehemently, Jack said, looking very solemn, but there it was. Nothing but work work work. He doubted that they would ever see the eighteen-hole championship golf course, the eight clay and eight all-weather tennis courts, the Olympic-size swimming pools indoor and outdoor, the well-stocked bar (and well-stacked waitresses, yak, yak—oh come on, honey,

where's your sense of humor, he said) and luxurious suites
with gold-plated fixtures on the bidets. She had caught a
glimpse of the conference-site brochure in his attaché case.
"It's a dump," he said. "You know how they beef up those
publicity pictures."

"Secretaries going?" she asked, her back to him at the
kitchen sink, slouching, a gesture of unconcern; and will
Miss Schaeffer be there? she didn't ask.
Jack's warm eyes always cooled when she tried to clutch
at a truth in his life. Truth or what her unfettered imagina-
tion conjured up. She didn't always know what was solid
intuition or the fiction of her mind when it concerned Jack
and the boys. Maryann had managed to elude her practical
parents' Calvinism through a passion for mystery novels.
Lord Peter Wimsey, Albert Campion, Hercule Poirot, Jane
Marple and Sam Spade. They convinced her that life could
not possibly be as simple as hello and goodbye and how was
your day, dear.
"A few, one or two, I think," Jack said carefully. "There's
a lot of paper work at these things."
She said she thought she ought to stay home and do some
work too (she was head of the volunteer drive at the hospital), and George had called her about putting together
the hymnal supplement before September. George was Pastor
Wollsetter, who had come to the First Presbyterian Church
without a tie three years ago and immediately went into re-
hearsal of a teenage production of Godspell. ("Light of the
World." "You are the . . ." Clap, clap, clap, clap! The
elderly members of the congregation obediently clapped and
gazed, stupefied, at the ebullient youngsters, the Mansfield
boys among them, who rattled up and down the aisle with
tambourines, painted faces and striped knee socks. A boy,
naked except for brief, cut-off jeans, splashed the parishioners
with a wet sponge as he cried, "God save the people!" George
also sent out a chatty God-loving newsletter which included
an outline of that week's sermon to help all follow "where he

was coming from." Maryann's mother, whose grandfather came from upstate New York to settle in the Ohio Valley soon after the Civil War, said she gave thanks to Jesus daily that she no longer lived in Chagrin Falls.)

"Maryann." Jack sighed. Then, "Honey, do what you like. I don't want to push you into anything you don't want to do."

The boys, she said; didn't he think someone ought to be home in case the boys needed them?

"For what? They're at camp. They don't even remember we exist."

"Let's call them."

"We just drove them up there a week ago, Maryann." She exasperated him. "Okay, let's call them."

They interrupted a Frisbee tournament and John, the elder, asked, "What do you *want?*" Maryann said she might go to New York for a few days and what did he think and he said, "Great. Send me more stamps before you go."

Tommy, the younger, had no opinion about New York and wanted her to send him his good-luck T-shirt.

"You don't have a good-luck T-shirt."

"Well, send one. I'm trying out for shortstop."

"Any woman would grab the chance," Jack said, finally, over coffee, having eaten his dinner ferociously. She and Ginny could shop, he said, go to the theater, shop, catch up on old times. His cousin, Joe Westcott, would take her out to a show, she could call his aunt Ella, who was still able to get around, and what the hell, treat her to a concert and dinner and take her shopping. Jack was full of suggestions.

He would feel so much better (about what? Maryann wondered) if he knew she was having a good time. "Let's call Ginny, see what she says."

"Maybe she's away," Maryann said.

But Ginny answered the phone with cries and gurgles. "You're coming to New York, ohhhhh, that's so hmmmmmm, I'm absolutely ahhhhhh. Of course you'll stay with us,

shshshsh, if you don't I'd be completely oughghgh."
"Well?" Jack asked. "Is it all set?"
"I'll think about it." She glared at him.

Maryann's mother called; Mrs. Morrison always seemed
to sense when not to call and called.
"Mother?" Unaccountably Maryann reverted to her adolescent questioning, her young life an eternal doubt. "Jack
has a seminar to go to at that new conference center and
wives aren't invited? So I thought I'd visit Ginny in New
York? Just a quick little trip?"
Her mother's voice blanched, a white sound of anxiety.
Mrs. Morrison's sister Louise had once been a missionary
espousing the Presbyterian cause in a leper colony near
Léopoldville. Now *that* was a noble journey. Going to New
York was plain silly (substitute dangerous) and Ginny's husband wasn't one of her favorite people. She was not a prejudiced woman (could anyone call her a prejudiced woman?),
but she found it hard to forgive Ginny for marrying an
R.C. and, furthermore, converting.
Then Mrs. Morrison reached Jack at his office. She didn't
know any woman in Chagrin Falls who went to New York
for a quick little trip, she told Jack. Described that way, it
sounded obscene. Maryann was a decent Christian woman,
a mother and wife, and should be protected and didn't Jack
agree? Waiters, wrong directions, the advances of inap-
propriate men. Certainly Maryann's father would expect it
as a given, she said, calling up the late Dr. Morrison from
his untimely grave, God rest his soul. (Maryann had sung
middle high soprano in the First Presbyterian Church
Chancel Choir since she was eighteen. "Behold! a Stranger
at the door . . . He gently knocks, has knocked before . . .
O lovely attitude! . . . He stands with melting heart . . ."
And her mother, catching her young daughter's dreamy
eyes as she sang ". . . with melting heart . . . ," said later,
"I hope you don't forget, Maryann, that you sing of Christ
and in church you are in the presence of the Lord.")

"Surely you can persuade your president to permit wives to attend, Jack. There must be recreational facilities there and Maryann will be no trouble at all."

That night Jack went to bed without speaking to Maryann.

Harper's Bazaar once listed a Phobia Dictionary between pages of Oscar de la Renta and tips on how to highlight sunken eyes. Maryann was surprised to find herself delineated by a simple suffix. In the A's alone she recognized aerophobia and agoraphobia; then there were two she never before identified: nyctophobia, fear of night, and ceraunophobia, fear of thunder. She detected a touch of tropophobia—she didn't always like making changes—and hoped her children didn't have arachibutyrophobia, fear of peanut butter sticking to the roof of the mouth.

But there was no doubt that one of the major phobias was decidophobia. In the following weeks should she or shouldn't ·she go to New York became a raging debate. It had to win some kind of prize for endurance alone. There were ninety-two dollars in telephone charges and plane reservations on different days respectively, each confirmed, canceled and re-confirmed at least once. She discussed it with her brother in Phoenix; three friends at different times and in private consultation; semipublicly at a formal dinner party for twelve; with the garage attendant at the hospital; with the aged clerk at Buster Brown Shoes who always repeated to John and Tommy the story of fitting the first pair of shoes on baby Maryann and how he used to tickle her toesies and John never failed to remark as they left the store, "That guy makes me puke."

She exhausted herself with lists of pros and cons. The con list was short and to the point. Too hot; prefer with Jack; plane crash. The pro list had optimistic appendages of what to take including shoes and handbags, and these lists were subdivided into other lists of clothes to be dry-cleaned, washed, ironed, etc. Also, Things to Do, such as milkman/

mailman notify, cat to B., dog to kennel, Lollie/plants, call
Eleanor take bridge, Sally comm. mtng will reciproc., call
camp gv alt. emerg #, gynec. appt.

It would serve him right if she met someone in New York.
Maryann was being slid down along the cold white paper
covering her gynecologist's examining table, propped in the
stirrups, wearing shoes and a chaste white sheet. It was her
annual checkup and Dr. Clarkson's nurse, Maryann's childhood friend and medium alto in the choir was humming
"Then the gates will open wide" as she adjusted Maryann's
knees. She had just said, "Golly, Maryann, my husband
would kill me if I even thought of going to New York. He'd
be afraid I'd be raped or maybe Mick Jagger or somebody
like that would sweep me off my feet and I'd never come
home. Oh Lord, Maryann." And she choked on her laughter.

Why wasn't Jack concerned that Mick Jagger would
ravish *her?* Well, it would serve him right if she did meet
someone. A divine man, witty, very charming. And she
too would be divine, witty and very charming. He'd be a
physicist from Berkeley or a visiting concertmaster from
Vienna or a classicist from Oxford. There would be a disturbing mutual attraction and she would know that he knew
that she knew that he knew . . . ("Maryann, are you all
right?" the nurse asked.) What would Jack say then, would
he be so willing to send her to New York? With a dried-out
diaphragm?

Her gynecologist didn't believe in the pill and ever since
Jack's vasectomy her diaphragm had been tucked away in
its zippered plastic bag, fossilizing on the top shelf of a closet.
After Jack returned from the urologist's office, walking very
warily, he urged her to throw it away, they would make it a
celebration, he said, a bonfire burning over the barbecue,
and then they would break open a bottle of champagne. The
implication being, as she viewed it later, that he was now
free to not impregnate any willing female in or out of Ohio

and there was no question about whom *she* would be sleeping with. Sterile Jack. Jack was the only man in the Chagrin Falls Rotary to have a vasectomy. One-upmanship.

Where was she? Oh, yes, the concertmaster from Vienna. Well, of course she wouldn't need a diaphragm in New York. Should she have kept it cleaned, lubricated, powdered, ready? Was that what one did? It was a matter only of curiosity. Sneak into a bathroom, wash it, insert it? Is that what women are carrying in their tote bags? Jelly, powder, inserters, douche bags? ("Did that hurt, Mrs. Mansfield?") She would have to bring her decongestion pills in case she fell asleep after . . . ("Mrs Mansfield, are you sure—?") Her snoring medicine, the boys called it. She had started to snore in the last few years and Jack, after nights of moving in with John or wearing his underwater earplugs to bed, begged her to go to a doctor.

"It's not the snoring that bothers me, honey," he said kindly, "it's the rhythm. It's so uneven, it drives me nuts."

The doctor had gasped and snorted with laughter and Maryann also did a few little ha-ha's, just to show him what a good sport she was.

The prescription worked rather well, two pills before bedtime and Jack was delighted. Only the boys were disappointed. "We told all the kids you were going to have your snorer cut out," Tommy said.

She was preparing a serious pro list, beginning to believe in New York, when Ginny called.

"Maryann baby, I was so wheeeee about your coming and now I feel completely whooosh. Ralph just told me he has to go to Italy for a week and I think I'll go with him. On one hand I feel absolutely oooowheee and on the other hand I feel totally yeough. Know what I mean? He says I should stay and do the town with you which would be oodles but you don't know my Ralphie, a week in Rome alone and he's liable to, you know, oomph like anything."

Maryann didn't know who would want to oomph like

anything with Ralph other than Ginny, who once had been wooed by a thinner, more hirsute and taller Ralph. Marriage had definitely fattened, balded and shortened him. However, she groaned and gargled with Ginny, told her of course she had to do what was best, and Ginny said of course Maryann had to stay at the apartment anyway and they would see each other at Christmas when Ginny and Ralph came to Ohio to visit her family.

Maryann and Jack resumed the debate and finally Jack said, well, look at it this way, it should be a real good time having a penthouse apartment to herself, how often would she get such an opportunity? She said she guessed so. Now it was Maryann who was stabbing meanly at the mush they had made of chocolate-chip ice cream.

How dare he tell her to go to New York and have a good time? If she wanted to go to New York and have a good time it was for her to say, Why don't I go to New York and (ergo) have a good time? She would show him. Pushing her around, placing her like a golf ball on a tee and then whacking her out of sight until he was ready to find her again.

"All right," she said, shoving out into nothingness, spinning in a free fall, "I *will* go to New York and have a good time," and was so deeply hurt when he kissed her and said, loving her so much, yes, he did, "That's my girl. Do it! You'll have a fabulous time."

A fabulous time. What happened to good? She might have managed good, but fabulous? Fabulous was at best a gross exaggeration. What in life could be more fabulous than loving Jack and the boys and taking care of them and when they weren't all there together—exasperating, demanding—feeling incomplete? (She was a hummingbird, hovering in the air, in, around, with them.) She knew she was an anomaly in her own time: she didn't want to live her own life. Oops, she said it and hoped no one heard, people like Gloria Steinem, Kate Millett, Betty Friedan. What she really meant, what she thought she really meant, was that the life she was living—she had to word it carefully to herself—was exactly how she wanted to live her own life. (That was better.)

It was absurd to think she could choose one or the other. Her own self or her own self with Jack and the boys. They were welded to each other. That's how she fantasized them, welded with solder from a craft kit until they were a moving mass, lumbering in one direction, then another, first here, then there; in her kitchen their collective heads in the refrigerator and eight hands, forty fingers stirring the spaghetti sauce; in Jack's office, a crowd behind his desk, as with one mouth they dictated a letter to Miss Schaeffer; four bodies lined up in Tommy's classroom aisle, a familial computer programmed to divide twelve into 126 and getting the wrong answer.

They loved each other and that was the whole point, wasn't it? Why in all the tumultuous shouting about clitoral orgasms, vaginal orgasms, a clearly defined schedule of who washed the dishes on Monday, did no one mention love?

She had never left them. Certainly she never wanted to leave them. Maryann was convinced that everything was perfect the way it was, and if she left them even for a little while they would be lost. (She would be lost?)

Was Miss Schaeffer going to the seminar?

Ginny called from the airport before the flight to Rome to say live it up, Maryann honey. "Just whooo-wheee! Ciao, baby."

Maryann's mother called and told her to pray to the most merciful God and above all not to sit on strange toilet seats.

Standing against the building, Maryann studied the urine-stained luggage, fixing her eyes on her initials embossed in gold on red leather. M.M.M.

She was almost forty and still hated her name. She had collected two Mariannes in her childhood at Camp Tekahati Trails; Maryann, her sister-in-law, and Maryann, her godchild; Mariann, her college roommate's cousin; one Mary-anne who was her husband's first steady girl friend and was now married to Jack's best friend's twin brother and with whom Jack recalled their romance with gauzy delight.

("Remember your father yelling at us, it wasn't fat Pat next door trust me because you lost the top to your bathing suit and your old man was screaming holy cow remember when the boat capsized?" and "No, you're wrong, that didn't happen until August after we smashed the Chevy" and "Bob was going with Peggy that summer, Betsy came after, well maybe you're right, maybe it was Betsy" and "Never forget holy cow . . .")

And two Mary Annes, one a checkout girl at Pick-N-Pay and the other the librarian at the Bertram Woods branch of the Shaker Heights library.

In the dim light of night on East Seventy-eighth Street she knew she was maundering. Her father often cautioned her against this inclination. Dr. Morrison's Calvinism had been puritanical tempered by kindness and natural good humor. (One cocktail at the club on Saturday night and the same joke—"I'm really on a toot tonight.") Life was a direct confrontation and one did what one had to do. He never turned down patients, house calls, emergencies, and Maryann saw him seldom. He was a man who felt awkward in the presence of the drama of communion and was mollified by the practical use of supermarket white bread, which, a deacon of the church, he dutifully cut up in cubes for the ritual wafer. Naturally, he would tell Maryann, one is permitted to put aside a difficult problem and go back to it with fresh perspective, but he knew that she adapted this advice as meaning free-associate and hope for the best. He always worried about his bemused daughter and urged her to rise to the occasion, for God's sake, meaning it quite literally.

And what would he make of this occasion? Maryann wondered with some self-pity.

Only two hours ago (and what did "only" mean?) she had arrived at La Guardia Airport on United Airlines flight 432

for that fabulous time she would have, astonishment concealing all her phobias.

There had been warning signals which she had ignored.
For instance, on her way from the airport to Ginny's apart-
ment, the cab speeding between buildings lined up on
Queens Boulevard like disheveled sentries, she noticed that
the traffic was bumper-to-bumper in the opposite direction.
She asked the driver where everyone was going.

"Out, lady, outtatown. To Long Island. Everybody gets
out on Friday. Only the crazies are left, the poor shnooks
who have no place to go." He peered into his rear-view
mirror and saw her startled eyes. "Ooh," he said. "Sorry, lady,
no offense." He was silent awhile and then, placating, with
a simulated charm dredged from someplace hidden behind
his Hawaiian shirt, "Where ya from?"

Chagrin Falls.

Where?

Chagrin Falls, Ohio. Near Cleveland.

"Cleveland!" He knew Cleveland and chuckled, this man
from Brooklyn, and rolled a flaking cigar to the corner of his
mouth; veiny eyes offered a dull glimmer that could pass for
a twinkle. "Wow. Cleveland. Yeah, well, I guess anything's
better than Cleveland. Right?"

Wrong, she thought.

"Cleveland shmeveland what difference does it make where
you live as long as you got your health. Right? Looka me.
I'm a happy man. I drive a cab in New York and I feel great.
You think I'd be happier if I drove around in a Rolls-Royce
in Paris? No way. Money don't mean nothin'. It's your
health that counts. If you feel good then you're a rich man."

He grinned at her; it was a spectacular flash of dingy
yellow. He pulled up in front of the building on Seventy-
eighth between Park and Lexington and the doorman rushed
out to take her luggage.

"Well, thanks for getting me here," Maryann said cheerfully. The meter read $9.65 and she gave him a twenty-dollar
bill.

"You gotta be kidding. I don't have changea twenty. I just came out. Whaddya think I am, a bank?"

Maryann searched her wallet and found more twenties and one ten. She looked in her change purse: a nickel, a St. Christopher medal and two safety pins. She gave him the ten-dollar bill and told him how sorry she was but that was the best she could do and "Thank you so much," she said, daughter of Dr. and Mrs. Thaddeus Morrison.

"Same to you," he said. His voice rose, "I'm gonna buy my wife Chanel No. 5 with that thirty-five cents," and leaning across the front seat in case she couldn't hear him, "Whyncha stay in Cleveland where ya belong, ya dumb cunt?"

A little tremor went through Maryann's knees. She looked around, but the doorman was setting her bags down in the lobby. The only witness was a delivery boy on a bicycle who stared at her, then pursed his lips and made little kissing sounds. Maryann hurried into the building.

"You're Mrs. Crawford's friend from Detroit?" the door-man asked her. Maryann thought about it and then decided that indeed she was.

"They left the keys for you."

Dependable Ginny, old college roommate, cousin to one of the eight Maryanns.

On the fourteenth floor, Maryann put the key in the lock and it wouldn't turn.

When she rang for the elevator man, he couldn't open the door either. They called for the doorman; the superintendent was away for the weekend.

"Get a locksmith, break open the door," the elevator man said finally, going down to get a call on the fourteenth floor.

(What she didn't know was that Ginny Crawford had left a note with the superintendent, who gave it to the doorman on the day shift, who put it in the drawer of the breakfront in the lobby and forgot to mention it to the night man. The note said: Dear Maryann, the top lock jams occasionally! *Important!* Jiggle it up and down three or four times then turn very slowly to right again. Voilà! Entrez! Please water plants on terrace. Champagne in refrig for you. Hope you won't drink it alone! Ha! Ha! Enjoy!!! Oodles, Ginny and Ralph.)

The doorman was back and tried again. "Lady, I can't open it and I gotta go back downstairs. You better get a locksmith." But he wasn't sure she could find one on a Friday night in July. "And it'll cost you a pretty penny. Lotsa luck."

What was a pretty penny on a Friday night in July in New York? "Twenty-five dollars?" Maryann asked.

The doorman looked at her with pity. "You gotta be kidding. No way. A hundred dollars. More even. You want in, they'll charge." The elevator came back to get him and the doorman's voice floated up as they descended: "Did you hear that? Twenty-five dollars. A hick from Baltimore, don't know nothin'."

Maryann was aware of the moment of surrender, when inertia began to settle over her like a cumulonimbus. If she could exist in the corridor up against the wall for four days, eating minimally—a little yogurt, the plain and fruity kind such as strawberry, gooseberry, blueberry, apricot, apple, some granola, maybe a cookie with chocolate chips for energy —then she would go back and tell Jack and everyone in Chagrin Falls what a fabulous time she had in New York. No one would ever know.

(As it was, she was already becoming a legend. The doorman often related the story, years later, like a gold prospector recalling past splendors, sitting around in the furnace room, his feet up on the super's scarred desk: "Hey, remember the time that dame from St. Louis couldn't get into 14P?")

"So what're ya gonna do?" The elevator man was back.

Silently Maryann opened her suitcase, found her drip-dry green dress, a nightgown, a pair of panties, a bra. She was being watched attentively but Maryann didn't care. It was obvious to her now that nothing really mattered anymore. She shoved everything into her cosmetic case and dragged her luggage into the elevator.

She didn't want to go to a hotel. A friend's available penthouse was rational—chic and enviable even—but a hotel room for one, alone in New York, was totally unexplainable, especially to herself. Of course there was always Aunt Ella, but Aunt Ella's idea of fun was dinner at Schrafft's and a travelogue at Town Hall on the Masai tribe. She couldn't even call Joe Westcott. At the last minute Jack said, "Forget Joe this trip. He's waiting for his final divorce papers and you may wind up holding more than his hand."

When Maryann got down to the lobby she told the doorman she would go to the Waldorf-Astoria for the night. She was sure Jack would approve of the Waldorf.

Could she leave her things with the doorman until the next day?

"Now you're talkin', no sweat," he said, mopping his forehead. "We'll put everything in the baggage room. Pick 'em up anytime."

She wanted to call the hotel and he said, desperately, hell, she could go right down, they had to have a single or something. She said firmly, no, she wasn't leaving until she called first. Gloomily he sent her in the direction of a pay phone beyond a service door but having remembered the St. Christopher medal, the two safety pins and one nickel, she returned immediately to borrow a dime. (Mrs. Crawford sure could pick 'em. On the other hand, Mrs. Crawford was no winner either.)

Maryann found the Waldorf-Astoria number in a worn and soiled directory hanging by a cord near the phone. She dialed the E, the L, the 3, and then her finger slipped while dialing the first 0. She would start over again, Maryann thought. She hung up and waited for the dime to return. She scratched around in the coin box. She wiggled the hook. She punched the box.

Maryann walked through the lobby toward the front door. "Thanks," she said to the doorman, trying out the smile of a straightforward, secure, responsible and intelligent woman who had a devoted husband, two fine sons, a beautiful Williamsburg Colonial, a new white Chevy Caprice in her name and a few credit cards stashed away in the plastic sleeves of a green Florentine leather wallet.

"You lost the dime, right?" he said sadly.

"I'm fine, thanks, I'll just get my bearings and decide what to do. Thanks anyway," she called again cheerily to no one at all and with no cause for gratitude.

As soon as he disappeared her lips furled. "Dumb creep," she muttered. "Shit on a stick." It hadn't always been her idea of a *mot juste* but Maryann was the mother of two boys, one fourteen, the other ten.

That was when she placed herself carefully against the building. The doorman came out again and hovered under the blue-and-white canopy, whistling a tuneless song and gasping on a cigarette hidden in his cupped hand. He took some time to brush off a few pieces of lint from his grease-limned black trousers with its red satin trim like a leer down the side of each leg.

At a discreet distance he called, "Lady!" Another day, another nut. "I can get you a taxi, go to some hotel, plenty hotels in New York. Go someplace." He meant it for her own good.

Go back to Chagrin Falls where she belonged. Take the next plane out. There must be a regular schedule of planes leaving for home. She could be there in two hours, door to door, get off the plane at Hopkins Airport, get into her car, drive out of the parking lot to Route 71 East to 90, to 271 and the Gates Mills exit, off at Route 422, another left and pull into their driveway on Falls Road, into her own house, her own bed, her own pillow, rest her tired body on the fresh garden pattern by Wamsutta . . . She could go to church on Sunday in time for Pastor Wollsetter's sermon announced on the lawn sign in plastic letters: "NEXT TO SALVATION A GOOD MOTHER IS GOD'S SWEETEST SMILE FROM HEAVEN."

"Why don't you let me get you a cab." The doorman tried a new cajoling voice, warm and helpful.

Maryann knew she couldn't bear to leave this place where

desperation had become something familiar to cling to. What would her mother say? (Reminding Maryann that one did not leave home without car keys, a previously arranged appointment, the correct address, mouthwash, the King James Bible—having rejected the new Good News version—and the determination to be absolutely correct in all things. Certainly not to call on the Lord as in help! help! since one should learn to do it all on one's own.) And Jack? (Holy cow, can't you pick up a phone, Maryann, and make a simple reservation?) Well, you're not here, Jack, so I don't care what you would say. And what's more, I'll punish you by never telling you what happened. Years later when we're old, I may tell you. If we ever see each other again.

"I'll just walk to the corner and take a bus or a cab, whichever comes first."

"Terrific," the doorman said, "you do that." He greeted a tenant, "Hot night, Mr. Buhlenbaum," and followed him into the lobby. Maryann waited a minute, deeply inhaled some polluted air, exhaled a tiny sad sigh, and went to look for him.

"No," he said. "Where would I get change of twenty? But I'll give you a dollar, that's all I can spare."

"I couldn't take it."

"You don't understand, I'm not giving. Now you owe me $1.10. Do me a favor lady, take it and go to the Waldorf."

2

Lilyan closed her eyes and yielded up her body to the sooth-
ing heat that oozed through all the space around her until
the room felt like a warm, moist, spongy cushion pressing on
Lilyan's limbs, toes, tits, fingers, belly, neck, mind.

She stretched out her large full frame on the pine plank
bench and capitulated to the sensation of weightlessness.

God, it felt good. Oh, Jeezus, it was heaven. Chu-rist, she
needed it.

Friday night was a bummer. But she wasn't sorry. Like
she told Nick, it was worth nine o'clock closing Thursday and
Friday nights during the summer just to have Saturday off.
They made as much money those extra evening hours as they
would on Saturday. When she first suggested it Nick argued
with her, but what the hell did he know, it was the only
beauty salon he ever owned. Laundromats were his bag
(joke) and who knows what else.

(Don't tell me what else, she said to him quickly at the
beginning of their association. I don't want to know about
your other enterprises.)

But she couldn't take a chance so she proved the Saturday
business to him a couple of years ago by keeping open one
Saturday early in July and comparing the appointment book
against two late nights a week. Nick didn't have to know she
refused Saturday appointments, telling clients they were all
booked up. "See for yourself," she said to him, handing him
the appointment book when he drove over from Jersey for
his look-see. That's what he called his twice-a-month visits,
look-sees. He got the expression from his orthopedist when
he broke his leg a few years back and used to go every week

for a look-see. Nick said he slid on a wet leaf in his driveway but Lilyan was sure somebody broke it for him over there in New Jersey if you get her meaning.

(He was incorporated under the name of N & I, Inc. N for Nicholas and I for Iano. He lived quietly in Wayne, New Jersey, in a two-family frame house and he and his wife, Theresa, spent their days in a laundromat, submerged in the odor of wet wash, folding other people's laundry and retrieving Cokes and packages of Oreo cookies from the back of the vending machine that chronically broke down at least four times a week. The most exciting thing that ever happened to Nick was when he slipped on some wet leaves in his driveway one October morning and broke his leg in two places. His only vice was the beauty parlor. He bought it through an ad in the Newark *Star-Ledger* with a little money he had saved and hidden from his wife. Lil was working there at the time and he made her the manager. He looked forward to his look-sees; all those women, their brassiere straps showing, half-slips, bulges of flesh and the air sweetened by lotions, dyes, sprays and femaleness. On those nights he amazed himself and Theresa.)

Lilyan could do hair, facials, manicures, pedicures, massages, coloring, cuts—the works, if she had to. Even though she was the manager, she still had her regular customers. She wore space shoes at the shop. That was the only thing she hated about the beauty business. Sometimes she thought she'd never make it to Roseland, but she always did and once on the dance floor, leave it to Lil, she felt like a million bucks.

She wriggled her toes and flexed her arches. Was this to be her life's condition—tired feet? Well, so what? It could be worse. Her brother Eddie was the one they sent to college; they couldn't afford to send two of them. That's what Pop said, but Lilyan knew the real reason was she was just a girl. Get a good job, he said, be a secretary, a typist, a bookkeeper. Finally they compromised and sent her to beauty school. (She didn't want to go to college anyway, she just wanted to cause

a little aggravation in the family for a while; let Eddie feel
guilty, why should he always get everything?)

The truth was, she had always wanted to be a beautician.
Even when she was a kid she loved doing people's hair, finding new styles for them, putting makeup on them, changing
how they looked. She even taught her clients how to do
their own makeup. ("You've got a round face, adorable, but
you want to slenderize it just a teeny bit so what you do is this
—watch me closely, here, hold the mirror—you take. . . .")
Once a guy said he could get her a job with the movies as a
makeup artist. They dated for a month, screwing every night.
He didn't get her the job but she never really expected him
to; she kind of liked the screwing part. She could do it all
day. Makeup and changing people's hairdos. And not that
she wanted to sound conceited, but she felt that people really
liked her. They told her their problems, the things people
tell you—and by the end of the day not only did her feet
hurt but her head ached with I-said-to-hims and he-said-to-
mes. But she prided herself on never confusing one woman's
trouble with another and always remembered to ask the following week (most of her clients were regulars, very few off
the street)—"So what happened?" And the client would say,
"Well, you won't believe it. . . ." Rhoda, the receptionist,
hidden behind her high front desk, would catch Lilyan's eye
and run her finger across her throat. But Lilyan didn't feel
that way. Lilyan's philosophy was that people were people.
And how could you tell them you didn't care? Lil knew
whose husband was sick (one kidney and that one going and
every cent went for dialysis and the lousy doctors); sleeping
around (and brought home you know what so that his wife
was so embarrassed for the doctor she could have died); un-
employed (she worked and he drank for a living and that's
not to say he wasn't a helluva nice guy); a wonderful person
(in all their married life he never said no to anything); a
bastard (that bastard); whose kid was a straight A (but he
never had a girl friend); dropped out (the boy calls once a
week always from another town, he's breaking his parents'

hearts); going steady (he's—a fella; she could do better); whose mother was a pain in the ass with a special diet (she can't eat this, she can't eat that); whose boy friend was going back to his wife (the shithead said he couldn't afford a divorce, after eight years, would you believe the nerve of the guy?); whose father was dying in an old age home (blind, his feet in a puddle of his own urine).

Lilyan yawned and sat up. She yawned again. One yawn always led to another she noticed and just seeing a person yawn or even saying the word yawn made her want to yawn.

"Yawn," she said aloud, and then yawned. She laughed and yawned again, letting free an exhaled bark. It had to do with oxygen, she decided; she really would like to know. She ought to talk to a scientist specializing in yawns. She didn't know any scientists; Sid was the smartest guy she ever knew. (Her brother Eddie didn't count. With Eddie it was always a kibbitz or a putdown gag.) How come she never asked Sid about yawning in the six years they were married? Because you think you know everything, big shot. Because you thought he thought you knew everything. That was a laugh. Because you wanted him to *think* you knew everything. But of course he didn't; whatever Sid was, he was no dope.

He treated her sneeringly, sometimes sublimated, sometimes a roaring outraged cry: "You're dumb. You're just a dumb cunt. How could I have married such a dumb cunt? How could I let you talk me into it?"

Talk him into it? That's a crock. Right from the beginning she told him she wasn't mental. But she was twenty-three with hot pants (wet underwear all the time: one feel, one *tup* and she was juicy). The first time she hadn't bled or hurt or anything, just squealed like a stuck pig and that was it. And Sid was a virgin—would you believe a twenty-three-year-old virgin?—skinny and pale, not even her type, with a 148 I.Q. He had begged her, moaning, fiddling with her nipples like they were radio dials and his fly stained through, he couldn't hold it in. And then he put his magna cum laude baccalaureate diploma under the pillow in her girl friend

Sylvie's apartment where her mother thought she was just sleeping over and they spent six months mounting each other. He mounting her, she mounting him, over and under and inside and outside and up and down and sideways and below and above like two becrazed Cossacks doing their tricks on horseback at dress parade for the Tsar.

When they eloped to City Hall they sent his parents a telegram (they had wanted him to be a lawyer) and when the messenger delivered it, the father threw the kid down the stone stairs (unencumbered of wife and children) of the old apartment building in the Bronx (Sid was an only child). They wouldn't talk to the newlyweds for a year (they had been prepared to sacrifice everything to see him at the bar) and his mother threatened to kill herself (and married to the daughter of some wealthy) with a knife (and Jewish judge).

Lilyan fulfilled one of her mother-in-law's requirements at least. She fed Sid, although never to the full satisfaction of his mother. Lilyan prepared his steak rare exactly as his mother always did, accompanied by mounds of mashed potatoes with volcanic pools of melted butter. She baked noodle puddings drenched in heavy sweet cream and strewn with cinnamon and raisins and roasted crisp whole chickens in the sappiness of oranges and honey. Sid's skinny sharp-edged frame disappeared in an unexpected pale pudginess. Even his pinched features grew fuzzy at the edges. He became a shoe salesman by day and went to law school at night. It would take maybe six, seven years to finish but Lilyan was determined to make him a lawyer (she'd show his parents) and, incidentally, herself a lawyer's wife (she'd show her father and her brother Eddie).

But after a few years she got bored. She wouldn't admit it to anyone but that was the truth. Life with Sid was boring. The initial thrill of his brain (and the old raspberry to her smartass brother Eddie) was over. I.Q. shmique, life with Sid was boring. Even fucking became boring and he began to smell like shoe leather.

After it was all over she told everyone that the main reason for the divorce was that he made her feel like nothing, always belittling her now that he was a lawyer. That was true, but there was the other reason which she was too ashamed to admit: all that intellectual stuff bored her. Torts, quasi, intestate, force majeure. She tried, but after a while she didn't know what the hell he was talking about. So she would come home from work, prepare dinner, they would eat, then Sid would sit in the kitchen and study. Or she would come home from work and do the dishes that he left in the sink before going to school. Eventually she was relieved on the nights he was out so that she could slide into bed around eight-thirty with a telephone and *TV Guide* and not feel guilty.

With the television turned low, the moving figures were good company while Lilyan called a friend. "Well, how did it go? Did you tell him what I told you to? See? I knew he'd back down, didn't I tell you? That's the way you have to deal with a guy like that, it's just human nature."

A friend called Lilyan: "Hello? What's the matter? Uhuh. No kidding? Yeh, yeh, yeh. Look, if it were me I'd go right to the doctor. You have nothing to lose and everything to gain. Don't be scared, he'll tell you it's nothing. I had a friend with the same symptoms, turned out to be nothing at all. I don't remember, piles, something like that, nothing."

Her friends said they didn't know what they would do without her, she should have been a psychiatrist. Once she had three cases all at the same time: a divorce, a hysterectomy and a job change. Sometimes she heard herself talking and thought she sounded more like a coach before the big game. Yea Betty, yea Rhonda, you can do it, you can win, go, go, go! They followed her advice and then reported back. They told her everything for fear that if they left out the smallest detail it might change some important nuance and then Lilyan wouldn't be able to make the right diagnosis or prescribe the appropriate treatment.

When Sid came home from school he screamed with high-pitched sarcasm, "Who do you think you are, Anna Freud? Get off the fuckin' phone and read something for a change!"

He told her to read Jung and Adler, Proust and Oliver Wendell Holmes. Instead she read books on astrology and true romances and traded paperbacks with a fourteen-year-old kid down the block. They'd meet every few weeks on the corner of Eighty-second Street and First and dig into each other's shopping bag. Sid caught her once and walked right by murmuring, "I don't know you."

Once she decided to take a course at the New School for Social Research without telling Sid. Psychology. Maybe it wasn't too late. Even grandmothers were getting degrees these days. On the day she was to go to her first class she had Iris at the shop do her hair in a windswept schoolgirl style. She left fresh fruit in sour cream in the refrigerator, Sid could eat it any time he came home. She told Sid she was going to a hairdresser's conference at the Americana Hotel and took the bus down to West Twelfth Street. It was the first night of fall classes and the entrance was jammed with people. Lilyan was terrified; her mind went completely blank. She joined a crowd standing in the middle of the lobby gazing up at a huge board on the wall, the kind you saw in train stations. On it were lists of courses, names, numbers, rooms, written in chalk. She searched the unfamiliar information and finally, with a tremor of relief, she found her course number. Next to it, under "Room," it said CANC. Where the hell was CANC? Why couldn't it be a regular room number like 523 or 308?

A guard in a uniform stood in the middle of the lobby; Lilyan approached him and managed to shout over the head of a gray-haired woman wearing basketball sneakers, a long woolen skirt and an army jacket with an Engineer Corps insignia.

"Where is CANC?" Her voice disappeared in the din. The guard's head, pivoting above his collar ("Take the elevator to the left," "Across the garden to the next building," "One flight up on the balcony"), finally revolved toward Lilyan.

"One flight down." Or something like that.

By now she was five minutes late and she pushed her way through a huge heavy metal door and clattered down the stairs. She faced a corridor of doors: Men, Women, Do Not Enter. No CANC. In desperation she flung open one of a double door and walked into an auditorium. About seven people cluttered around a woman sitting on the edge of a stage. The woman was saying: "In this sort of thing you must remember that you will get out of it only what you put into it." Aha! thought Lilyan, exactly what she told Sylvie on the phone the other day. She moved down front and joined the others and stayed long enough to find out she was in Beginners' Zen and tiptoed out when everyone was doing their za-zen.

Upstairs she approached the guard again and heard a man say, "I see on the board that my course has been cancelled, what do I do about a refund?"

Lilyan never applied for her hundred-dollar refund; she was afraid that Sid would pick up the mail before she did and then she'd have to explain and she didn't want to explain it to Sid. (She knew in her head that she didn't have to explain anything to Sid but in her heart she knew her big mouth would tell him everything.)

Fourteen years now she didn't have to explain anything to Sid or apologize or plead/beg: "Tell me that you love me." Once it had come out: "Tell me that I love me." He never let her forget it.

It took six years for the scales to fall from her eyes, she told her friends. And just so it shouldn't be a total loss she weighed herself, and found she had gained forty-five pounds living with Sid.

Bye bye Sid. When the divorce became final she really didn't love him any more but she cried anyway for when she used to love him.

* * *

Lilyan leaned forward, gyrating her shoulders. Perspiration poured from her head and down her cheeks like tears. "Ah, my kopf runneth over," she murmured.

3

Maryann walked toward Lexington Avenue nervously aware of shadows and footfalls, muggers and rapists. This was New York; it was night; it was dark; she was alone. She tried, half-heartedly, to conjure up the civility of a Dorothy Sayers mystery but it felt more like Mickey Spillane and she never did like those seedy motel murders.

The street was almost empty except for the presence of a few lights behind the curtains and blinds of townhouses. Maryann knew people were there, hermetically sealed off from disaster by air conditioners bolted to windowsills. They were eating, drinking, loving, laughing. She couldn't imagine anyone in those lofty, softly lit rooms crying or feeling miserable, depressed, suicidal.

Two women came out of a brownstone, all clickety clackety down the front stairs. They were wearing jeans, tie-dye shirts, firm buttocks, buoyant breasts, tennis racquets, overnight bags and smiles for the men in the Volvo waiting for them at the curb.

Tears tickled Maryann's eyes. She wanted to say to those women, Listen, I am not one of your lonelies or crazies. I am not a shnook. Come to Chagrin Falls where I am, among other things, Secretary of the Friends of the Chagrin Falls Branch of the Cuyahoga County Library, and see that I am you and the only reason I am here in New York alone is to have a fabulous time. Instead she walked past them silently, looking quite elegant and dignified in her fine 100 percent Indian cotton pantsuit and wondered if they saw her slip on a Milky Way wrapper, making a clumsy dip, arms and hands spastically splayed for balance, before she hurried around the corner.

She stood at the sign that said "BUS STOP—NO STANDING." If she had it to do all over she'd be an English major and rewrite the city's signs for her thesis. 9:40 P.M. on her neat Bulova. Only a few cars passed and two cabs, both occupied. Where was everybody? The dollar probably wouldn't get her down to Forty-ninth Street in a cab anyway and she'd rather die (". . . rigor mortis had already set in when they found an unidentified woman's body standing upright against the No Standing sign on Lexington and Seventy-eighth Street . . . ") before she'd offer another cab driver one of her twenty-dollar bills.

Her intangible sense of desolation materialized in the day's other leftovers around and under her white clogs. An apple core, a flattened cigarette butt, a wad of chewed gum, a torn advertisement like an aborted cry: "   for the children we boycott   grap   no compre   uvas! nited Farm Worke   AFL-CI   " A seductive message: "Why Be Un-happy? Madame Flora Will Advise on Love, Money, Mar-riage, and Will Help You Overcome Enemies and Stumbling Blocks. She Warns Gravely, Suggests Wisely, & Explains Fully." (In the distance a growl of thunder.) Across the street the windows of a brick building were hammered shut with sheets of metal that shimmered eerily above the streetlight. The pizza place was closed; so was a coffee shop, an optician, a discount drugstore. All the windows and doors were pro-tected by iron bars. Supposing she was hungry or needed an aspirin or a pair of glasses? If Jack were here he'd say it was an adventure, terrific, hey, tell them what happened to you in New York, honey. She'd dine out on it. God she was hungry, just noticing the grumbling complaints in her stomach while a belch rose to her throat, the sandwiches served on the plane a distant and indigestive memory.

Maryann looked up the avenue; there was a rise a block above and she could see nothing at all beyond it, no glaring headlights of a bus to take her to the Sodom and Gomorrah known as downtown. Where was the bus, why hadn't one come along yet? Maybe they didn't run after a certain hour.

She was relieved when a young woman joined her at the bus stop. Maryann watched her remove a stick of gum from its wrapper, crumble the paper and toss it on the sidewalk. Rather than being critical, Maryann was reassured by the careless gesture. The woman seemed at ease in the night, alone, as though the caged storefronts were a reasonable landscape. A waitress. Probably going home from her job at a neighborhood luncheonette or starting the late shift at a restaurant. She seemed preoccupied.

(The woman had just awakened and was on her way to an apartment at Forty-ninth Street near Second Avenue where she would have a drink, make a few telephone calls and change into a brief green dress and large loop earrings. Then she would put on lipstick, mascara, eyeliner and saunter down to her usual spot on Lexington and Fiftieth Street opposite the Waldorf. And if that fat motherfucker showed up again she'd triple the price and if he didn't like it he could shove it, but not in *her* ass.)

Maryann tried to catch a glimpse of her left hand; was she wearing a wedding ring? Was there a husband waiting? It's ten o'clock; does your husband know where you are?

Maybe Jack was trying to reach her at Ginny's this minute. She should have been there by now. Was he sick with worry? On behalf of his sickening worry her stomach muscles tensed; oh, poor Jack, what was she doing to him? Guilt absorbed all else for a brief moment. But then she knew he wouldn't try to call her until around Saturday to see if she was having a fabulous time and she shifted easily from guilt/care to anger/resentment.

She had never been able to teach Jack the fine art of panic. Although, in all fairness, it was rare that he had to worry about her or the kids. Somehow she was always where she should be, and Jack knew that she always knew where the boys were. Once she made Jack promise that if, for whatever reason and never mind what reason, she wasn't around anymore to worry, he would assume the role of worrier. He promised, but added that as a worrier he could never live up to her standards. Hers was a richer stress than his.

If Tommy was late five minutes Maryann imagined him run over by a bus or surrounded by vicious bullies and unable to escape. John's smallest cut was examined daily for signs of the white shadow of infection. Both boys grew up learning how Isadora Duncan died ("But who *is* she?" they wanted to know) and to this day they still tucked in their long winter scarves. And when Jack was delayed while out late with a client or driving home alone from a poker game, she seemed to spread out her fears as though at a macabre feast and gobbled them up.

What was she afraid of? That Jack might fall down a hole somewhere and never be seen again, fantastic him, lost forever? Yes. Or he'd be mugged, even among the fine topiary boxwood of Chagrin Falls? Yes. Or he'd pick up a hitchhiker on South Woodland—although she told him never never to pick up hitchhikers—and at the point of a gun be forced into that lovely hidden wooded section of holly and rhododendron, dogwood and white birch where he'd be robbed, beaten, left to bleed to death? Yes. Or—she often rearranged the narrative if it seemed illogical even to her—he'd try to outwit the madman (the hitchhiker became a madman, an escapee from an asylum) and at that minute a description was being circulated on the two-way police radio but too late for Jack, too late. . . . Anyway, in the desperate tussle for the gun, the car would swerve and smash into an oncoming truck and Jack would be killed instantly. . . . Or not instantly and alive for a brief second, his words a burble in his dying throat, "tell Mmmmaaar . . . love . . . ?" Yes.

She told him, and believed it, that she could always sense if he was in danger. (When was the last time I was ever in *danger*, for God's sake? he asked, incredulous.) It was an ESP based on loving, she said. "And emanating from where?" he wanted to know, slipping his hand under her nightgown, searching, he said, for that extrasensory perceptive point that joined them as one.

And the nights he was out of town her friends knew that

all bridge games, all meetings, were to be held in her house because Jack always called her and she had to be home to receive the calls. Occasionally he would call long after midnight and she would be sick with worry (was he all right?) mixed with anger (what could he be *doing?*). One late night she reached a point of real rage: she was tired of caring so much, just generally caring so much. Loving was hard; it had to be easier not to love. But then she leaped toward the phone on the first ring, forgetting the worry, forgetting the anger, the insidious distrust (about what he might be *doing* and with whom) and cried, "It's you! Dear boy, you are everything to me." Isn't that wonderful?

Isn't that awful?

What a life, she thought as the Lexington bus seemed to swell up from nowhere and heaved itself to the curb.

Maryann handed the bus driver the dollar bill.

"Can't make change," he said. "Fifty cents or a token."

Sudden dismay made her whine and then beg: she would never bother him again if he would do it just this once, she promised.

"I can't, miss, even if I wanted to. We don't carry money. Too many ripoffs, it's all locked into the box."

"So what can I do?"

The bus driver told her he didn't know what she could do, that she was the third stiff he had that night and people like her burned his butt.

"I'll pay for her, let's go!" It was the nice girl from the bus stop. The driver shrugged, turned the wheel and pulled out into a red light.

Maryann stumbled up to her. "Thank you so much, but really, I'd rather you gave me change of a dollar if you have it."

The woman poked in her purse with one finger and found three quarters and three dimes. "I don't have a nickel. Be my guest."

Maryann said no (two hours in New York and already

owing strangers $1.15) and please just give her two dimes. Maryann held out the third dime at the same time the woman waved her hand magnanimously telling Maryann there would be more. Their hands met in mid-air and the dime rolled down the front step. The bus came to a jolting stop as Maryann scrambled to retrieve the coin.

"You crazy or something?" the driver screamed at her, and the woman shouted, "Leave it and let's go, I'm late for work!"

Maryann hurried to a seat in the middle of the bus (did the front or the back fall off in case of a crash?), her whole body busy with the feeling of mortification. Was everyone looking at her?

Actually only one person was looking at her, a man directly across the aisle. He was making strange sounds and opening his mouth wide in a joyless gold-capped grimace. She looked away, then up, considering carefully the series of ads running across the top of the bus that told her if she drank that brand of scotch she was not only wise but a beautiful person, socially superior and one of the elite. All this reassurance from a couple of dogs. The man was now smacking his lips noisily—kissing her? devouring her? Then he cradled his arms and his volcanic glare seemed to lock her in his embrace. The other people on the bus were looking out a window, reading a book, examining the tips of their shoes, cleaning out the wax in their ears. Maryann seemed to be the man's only hostage. He began to move his fingers skillfully, a sign language, eagerly telling her something she was sure she didn't want to hear. He also smiled a lot and to avoid his hypnotic spangly mouth Maryann forced herself to lower her eyes. They fastened at his creased crotch with its large, round, taut bulge. She turned her head swiftly and though she tried to concentrate on the "Jesus Saves" sticker pasted to the window, she remembered the time (it pounced on her brain before she could intercept the impulse) she sat in the dentist's chair with a pad and pencil in her lap. She knew after the first appointment that under the influence of nitrous oxide she was reaching either her most inner subconscious or was being contacted, through Dr. Sweigert's high-speed drill, by a greater power beyond with an apocalyptic message that would, at the very least, give her the answer to the universe.

On the third and last appointment, she kept a pad and pencil in her lap and prepared to scribble any astounding revelation from this interstellar news service.

"Open your mouth wider, Mrs. Dinosaur." Dr. Sweigert's voice seemed muffled by cotton swabs (could he actually have said that?) and she wrote haltingly the first thing that came to her mind in that finite second—even as the thought was slipping away.

The core of life is sex.

That's what she wrote: The core of life is sex.

She examined the scribbling surreptitiously as Dr. Sweigert made a few more stabs at the porcelain crown. Maryann Morrison Mansfield, was this the message? This solipsistic Freudian cant for, from, to someone who had not really given any personal thought to Freud since her sophomore year at Miami U.? Or to sex, for that matter.

That wasn't true and she'd put it another way: sex for the sake of sex. Pure sex. Only sex. (And that wasn't completely true either; she lied to herself quite a bit.)

Maryann's story went as follows:

She was a virgin when she married Jack. Be a good girl and you'll go to heaven, her father told her when she was three, and when she was fourteen her mother gave her marked passages in one of Dr. Morrison's medical texts, prudently leaving Maryann to read alone in the study. Then on the eve of her wedding, Mrs. Morrison cautioned her daughter not to have babies too quickly; unspoken: Jack should use a contraceptive.

She had never permitted anyone, even Jack, to go all the way. That was one of those old-time phrases. Making out was another. Once, her John, ten at the time, came home and said, smirking, too excited to keep the secret, that his classmate Glenn had made out with Claudia. Maryann's head was in the basement freezer looking for a container of turkey soup she had shoved to the back of the shelf, and when he said that she thought she would faint on the spot, keel over, possibly fracture her skull on a twenty-pound rib roast.

"Made out?" she screeched, instantly scaring up a pulsating knot in John's belly. (He shouldn't have told her, now she'll tell Glenn's mother and. . . .) "With Claudia, that nice little girl on Ardmore in the red brick house, *that* Claudia?"

Later, when she was more composed and realistic she asked, in conversational tones, "What do you mean when you say 'made out'?"

"Forget it," he said.

"I'm just curious."

"Make believe I didn't tell you anything."

"Okay," she said, hoping to disarm him.

"She let him kiss her."

Maryann laughed and laughed and John swore to himself he'd never tell her anything again. (And he never did.)

Having an affair, sleeping with, making out—what else?—there had to be more. At first the young Jack tried to reason with the young Maryann. "It's really a beautiful thing Maryann and I want you so much and I won't think the less of you how could I when I respect you so much and you mean more to me than any girl I've ever known I promise."

But back in 1958 she couldn't take a chance on promises, on getting pregnant, on statistics. It was said, mathematically speaking, that 51 percent of the female population of her class had carnal knowledge of and with 1.5 males. (Who was that half male?) Supposing the numbers were wrong and it turned out that she would be no. 6 of only fourteen non-virgins among hundreds who were still virgins?

After Jack proposed marriage, he, Jack, with what seemed to Maryann to be peculiar logic, stopped trying to score. (That was another one: to score. She was a ball. Score, balling, there was a joke somewhere.)

By then Jack had decided to be an actuary and was a

graduate student at Miami U., choosing to stay in Oxford, Ohio, where Maryann was still a senior. In his room or hers, in his '49 Chevy, at the golf course after dark. Where and when, the season nor the place didn't matter. They wouldn't go all the way of course but would grasp at each other, hands and mouths busy busy busy with ravening explorations. Long before they married they knew how the other felt and tasted and smelled and had manipulated each other to many noisy, satisfying orgasms. (Still Maryann was uneasy. She had always believed the Virgin birth to be allegorical and she wasn't taking any chances: in all of this maneuvering genital did not touch genital.)

When she and Jack stood triumphantly on the receiving line at the church where she had sung of melting hearts, their friends and family around them, her roommate, Ginny, who was her maid of honor, whispered in her ear in the guise of a kiss, "You made it, kid, you're married and you're still a virgin."

(Ginny was one of the fourteen nonvirgins; Maryann could hardly believe it, although she knew it for a fact. When they were in their junior year, Ginny said to Maryann, "I'm too blyuch, I mean, goughough, Maryann, I can't yuchch it anymore." She then spent the next two weeks in a deliberate search of the campus. She made Maryann help her too and they both brought back suggestions which they reviewed late at night, checking off names and devising a very simple code. A was physical attraction; B was mental attraction; C was availability. There were no complicating subtleties. Pete Stoller was B minus A; George Blakeley was C minus A and B; Jim Rieverman was A minus C. And so forth.

They had eliminated twelve names after intense discussions and some arguments and were down to five candidates when Ginny—without a word to Maryann or even codifying him first—chose a blue-eyed, mild-mannered teaching assistant in the economics department. She got herself invited to his single room in Mrs. Ketcher's boardinghouse at the edge of the campus, and when she bled all over the sheet the poor man jumped up, his penis renascent and pointed accusingly at her as he vowed, pitiably, that she would mend, would grow back together again and nobody would be the wiser. Ginny loved him for a few weeks and then grew tired of him.)

Maryann put on a new beige cotton going-away suit and teased and lacquered her bouffant hairstyle with the help of her bridesmaids, Ginny, her mother, her Aunt Louise. His ushers filled Jack with bourbon while he donned a pair of tan slacks and a blue blazer.

They left behind them Dr. Morrison, shamefully drunk for the first time in his life, and all the wedding presents (waffle irons, cocktail shakers, Spode china, Waterford crystal, electric clocks, pressure cookers) and flew to Hawaii, where, on their wedding night, they went all the way, made out and scored before appearing on the beach—pale, exhausted, shaken, suffering from charley horse and confusion—and holding their towels, suntan lotion and magazines.

In the first year they did it before breakfast, occasionally at midday and always at night. Jack, tenaciously, studiously, arranged ingenious tableaus that startled Maryann and they did it on beds, tables, sofas, floors, deck chairs; in showers standing up and in bathtubs lying down. In time she learned how to have an orgasm with Jack inside her (after years of clitoral manipulation) and she became a grunter at the moment of climax while Jack bellowed like a wounded bull. It put a strain on them when they visited his parents at the Peninsula cottage in Michigan with Mr. and Mrs. Mansfield sleeping discreetly on the other side of the thin plywood partition and Jack insisting it was okay. With each thrust the bed creaked against the wall and Maryann tried to contain her grunts. "Did you come?" Jack would ask hoarsely into her ear, not used to her silence. Once the bed really went thwack and awakened Mr. Mansfield. "Wha, wha, hey kids, you all right?"—and then there was a lot of shooshing from Mrs. Mansfield and Mr. Mansfield's soft chuckle.

When the boys were born her breasts were swollen with milk and hurt. A child cried just as Jack got on top of her. So weary she could barely make it from sofa to bed while waiting for Jack to come home. Late from the office. After Tommy's birth her doctor sewed one too many stitches and she was always tense, anticipating the pain. Jack tried to console her by singing his fraternity's version of "Sam, You Made the Pants Too Long" but she didn't think it was funny. In time "wear and tear" (yak, yak, Jack said) made it all right again. And Jack, fondling her until she was roused and ready and he was fast asleep.

He didn't snore.

They weren't swinging types. She didn't think they knew any. Where did all those stories come from? Somebody must be making them up. Imagine talking normally to a friend—"More salad?"—knowing they were doing what to whom and how they looked while doing it. She was glad not to know. (An oozy warmth was moving down from her groin and she was pressing hard on the bus seat. Did New York do that to you or was it a vaginal infection?) Besides, her friends didn't indulge in those kinds of confidences. Women in her British novels, for instance, were always saying outrageous things. "You know your Cecil crawls into Rosamund's bed and I say it's jolly good of you to still have her down for the fortnight." Or, "I've always told Derrick that sex is your downfall, Meg my girl. Scones?" Who would say things like that to each other?

Of course there were divorces, separations, undercurrents of minor scandals, but on a whole their group was a harmless one. Tim Best surprised her once, rubbing up against her while dancing at the club. It was deliberate; he wanted her to know he was hard. She was appalled by the discovery that it felt slightly crooked and on the way home that night she almost told Jack that Tim's thing was crooked. But what kind of news was that?

Jack came home from a business trip with the word *shtup*. Where did you hear that word? she wanted to know. But he

laughed and said it again, "Shall we shtup tonight?" Sometimes, "You feel like shtupping?" It became his new verb
transitive. She loathed the word. Where had he picked it
up? Who had taught it to him?

Maryann turned away from the Jesus Saves sticker and
knew that the man was looking at her again. He was making a loud sucking sound with his tongue against the gold-
capped molars. He scratched the bulge at his crotch.

Maryann grabbed her cosmetic case and clattered out the
exit door hoping she looked as though she knew exactly
where she was in the world.

4

Lilyan awakened with some confusion. She was stretched out on the bench, her sweating back imprinted by the pine planks. She had been dreaming about dancing with someone she called Sid but who resembled Lou. Or was it with someone called Lou who resembled Sid? She couldn't have been asleep more than ten or fifteen minutes but it felt as though she had returned from very far away.

She and this Lou-Sid Sid-Lou person were dancing. Actually, it must have been Sid (looking like Lou and what did that mean?) because she recalled the feeling of pushing him, not dancing at all really, but shoving him around the floor the way she used to with the real Sid when she thought she might still teach him how to dance. (Lou was a terrific dancer, but maybe the dream was symbolic and it was Lou she was pushing around, so to speak. It was too much to try to understand.)

When Sid agreed to go to Arthur Murray and paid for ten introductory lessons he resisted them too. For spite, Lilyan was certain. Sid was a spiteful man. During all those years of being married to Sid, Lilyan didn't dance. Maybe at an occasional wedding or a bar mitzvah and then if Sid did condescend to dance it seemed to Lilyan worse than not dancing at all. As a dancer, Sid was like an extension of their lives, unyielding, without joy. All around her couples were twirling and dipping and she ached to feel the music in the arms of someone who would change her into the dancing girl she knew she really was.

She took to dancing alone in front of the mirror when Sid wasn't home. It was like masturbation, but the hell with it, she was her own best partner. The night he walked out she cried, naturally, and got bombed drinking a half bottle of vodka and a pint of Seagram's. Then she fell asleep after vomiting all over the bathroom rug and her housecoat. The next morning, so sick she wanted to die, still she turned on the radio and danced and danced and danced. Alone. Me and my shadow. What she needed was a dancing man.

Lilyan stood up and did some stretching exercises. Touching her toes, her breasts swayed like elephant trunks. She couldn't afford to get stiff if she and Lou were going to try out at Joe's place Sunday night.

Babababa chachachacha babababa chachachacha pah chchch

Her big body glistening, she slid easily into a tempo. Her feet were motionless and she kept the rhythm with her hips and shoulders.

Chonkachonkachonkachonka

What would she have done without Roseland? One of her girl friends persuaded her to go after Sid left her.

It was a new world, Roseland. When she started to go there few people remembered it. It used to be big in the forties and fifties. But now they were doing movies and plays about Roseland, big deal, she knew about it before anyone else.

She met Lou there. For a long time he didn't talk, they would just dance until the orchestra played "The Party's Over." (She loved that song; even if the evening hadn't been anything much, the song made it seem as though it had all been grand.) The party was over and Lou would just kind of nod and walk away. Remove his arms from her body and leave. Funniest damned thing. A lot of guys at Roseland were like that. Twinkle-toed and tongue-tied. Anyway, she started to go on a regular basis, every Tuesday, Saturday and Sunday, and Lou was always there too. So one night they were really hot together and decided to enter the dance contest. The mambo. They won. And the rest was history. (Eddie said the rest was mystery.)

Lilyan always made sure people knew that Lou and his wife

were legally separated before he met Lil. Not just separated; legally separated. That was one thing with Lilyan, maybe she'd go out with a married guy once, twice, but that's all; she never got serious. She didn't want to hurt anybody. It was just that sometimes she used to feel abandoned by the rest of humanity and needed a reminder that she was a living breathing kissing fucking woman.

Lou was one sad guy when Lilyan met him. Only his feet were happy. No matter what Eddie said, she felt that she probably loved Lou. (Listen, who's Eddie? And what's love?) For no good reason, Eddie made it seem as though Lou was something she dragged home.

Like that dog she almost got mixed up with this morning. She was on her way to the shop when a big dog, a German Shepherd, started to follow her at Eighty-second and Second. It had a collar but it looked lost. People were avoiding it, slobbering and panting the way it did, and even Lilyan backed off when it got too close. Poor thing, somebody ought to call the police, she said to anyone passing by. It was Nick's day for his look-see and she didn't want to be late, otherwise she'd hang around and do something for that poor dog. Reluctantly she kept walking and wouldn't you know it, two blocks away there was a notice stuck on a lamppost. "Lost, female German Shepherd. Children heartbroken. Any knowledge of whereabouts please call above number or 19th Precinct." That was fate, right? What else? Lilyan couldn't remember whether or not the dog had balls (who looked?) but she hurried to her shop on Eightieth Street, repeating the number over and over. She got the door open, turned off the burglar alarm, grabbed the phone and dialed.

"Hallo?" A woman's voice answered.

"I think I saw your dog," Lilyan said, speaking quickly. The dog had turned a corner and could be down at the river by now.

"Who is this?"

"I'm a person who saw your dog."

"My what?"

"Your dog, your dog! Didn't you put up a sign saying you lost a dog?"

"Yeah. So?"

"So I think I saw it just now on Eighty-second and Second going east."

"The dog was found," the woman said, "and don't call again," she added before slamming down the receiver.

Lilyan helped the blind across the street, sometimes having to go out of her way like going uptown even though she was headed downtown or going east even though she was on her way west. Once she was going up Madison Avenue on the bus, it was around ten o'clock at night and she saw Paul Newman—get this, really Paul Newman—walking up the avenue with some guy. So she got off the bus at the next stop and pretended to be looking into a store window until he would catch up to her. All she wanted was to see his gorgeous blue eyes, that's all. She'd never dream of talking to him. Well, Lilyan's luck, a blind lady was on the corner tapping her cane, trying to cross Madison, and nobody was paying any attention. Aw, shit, somebody take her across. But nobody did. Lilyan had to run to the corner and walk her across. "Hi, nice night, may I help you across?" Lilyan believed in friendly conversation. By the time she got back to the other side of Madison, Newman had already passed by and was ahead of her and all she saw was his well-tailored tush.

She dropped coins in tin cups of the lame and the halt. "Here but for the grace of God . . . You can walk, I can't . . . Please help . . ." Mea culpa, mea culpa, clink-clink went the coins she dropped into the cups, sometimes her last quarters and dimes and then she was stuck for the correct change for bus fare. She took the offered grisly comic books or the no. 2 pencils, as a gesture to their self-respect. Sure she read the stories in the newspapers about some old man found dead in his room, a beggar, and under his mattress in old shoe boxes were fifteen bankbooks totaling

$367,000. Okay, she exaggerates—$15,670.92 and half those quarters hers. Sure they might be frauds and sometimes she tried to catch a glimpse behind dark glasses to see if there was a glimmer, a shrewd flash of sight. Or she would casually look behind as she passed to see if they were sitting on their haunches instead of being truly legless. But she gave anyway. If they were frauds then they were mocking the really disabled and it was their souls that were crippled, so what was the difference, was the way Lilyan looked at it.

"They're not cripples, it's a racket," her ex, Sid, used to say. But Sid had a chip on his shoulder so big he was lopsided from carrying it.

"Okay, okay, they're not cripples." She'd agree to anything he said at that point in their lives. (But supposing they are, she whispered into the crack of the closed bathroom door, softly enough for Sid not to hear.)

A raft complex. That's what Sid always said. "You have a raft complex," he used to tell her. "You're on a big, beautiful ship having a great time and down below you see someone on a raft. 'Are you in trouble?' you yell. Listen to me, Lilyan, I'm telling you something very important about yourself. 'Yes,' the person answers. 'Don't worry,' you yell back, 'I'll throw down a rope.' So you look for a rope and you can't find one. 'I can't find a rope,' you yell again. 'So what shall I do?' the person says because suddenly you're the big adviser. 'Don't worry,' you say, 'I'll come down and think of something.' So you dive off the deck of this big luxury liner where you're having such a swell time, and before you know it, Lilyan, you are on a raft drifting out to sea with a stranger."

Chubumchubumbum Chubumchubumbum chubumchubumbum

5

The street sign said East Fifty-sixth Street; her watch said ten sixteen. She had an overwhelming sense of being in an alien place at the wrong time. She might just as well be in Lenin Square in Budapest at nine in the morning. She made that up. She didn't really know if there was a Lenin Square in Budapest. But where in the universe was Lexington Avenue and Fifty-sixth Street?

If she walked seven blocks downtown would the Waldorf really be there? Yes, Maryann, there really is a Waldorf-Astoria. She saw a telephone alcove on the corner and hurried to it, aware of another rumble of thunder and another twinge of ceraunophobia. She was overcome by a teary anger against the city in general and Jack, Ginny, the doorman and her mother in particular.

Maryann found a last dime in her purse and tried to recall the telephone number.

"Waldorf-Astoria."

"Oh!" Maryann was genuinely grateful. "Would you have a room available tonight, please?"

"I'll connect you with reservations."

And then a voice with a British accent said: "This is reservations all agents are presently occupied you will be automatically connected as soon as an agent is free this is the only recording you will hear."

Maryann waited and was busy reading disturbing messages from other people ("Lick me" ballooning out of the mouth of a State Supreme Court Justice seeking reelection; "Bobby G eats shit for breakfast"; "Ada sucks") when she heard the operator ask for five cents for three more minutes and then some clicking sounds over which came distant words, "This is reserva—". And then silence.

She clawed the bottom of her handbag. There was a nickel goddamn it somewhere. No sooner had she said that word, there was a gash of lightning and seconds later thunder rolled over and around her. Then almost immediately large dollops of rain leaped and ricocheted off the pavement in a wild water ballet. Instantly she was drenched and her bra and panties outlined like Tommy's magic pad, the kind he got as a souvenir at the Buster Brown Shoe Store; he could choose a pad or a balloon and he always chose the pad.

It was all Jack's fault and she didn't care if she ever saw him again (lightning, clap of thunder). She slammed the phone down on its hook, hoping to rip it off the wall.

Health Spa, Capri, Health Spa. OPEN. The neon sign blinked at her halfway down East Fifty-sixth Street. She crossed Lexington Avenue against the light. She would stay there even if she had to sit up in a steam room until morning.

Maryann ran down the block, her hair plastered to her scalp, pursued by the echo of her clogs making squishing, squooshing sounds.

6

At first Lilyan didn't pay much attention to Maryann sitting opposite her, although the steam room was narrow and their knees almost touched. For a while she rotated her shoulders in wide circles, loosening the taut back muscles. Her breasts undulated sinuously, in and out, in and out, and she looked down at them. Knock wood, she really had good boobs. Big, but still firm even at forty-three. Maybe if she'd had some kids they'd be down to her *pupik*. (Too late for those kids, she thought, sad to feel almost relieved.) She began to knead the rolls of flesh around her waist, and looked critically at the woman lying so still on the bench.

"I can see you don't eat prune danish for breakfast," she said.

Maryann opened her eyes, pretending she had just awakened.

"Not a bulge on you," Lilyan said mixing envy and admiration until they blended into hostility, which then made her feel guilty so she hurried to compliment Maryann. "Everything in perfect proportion, breasts, hips, legs, you have a great body," she said with professional assurance as though Maryann had come for a consultation. "Look at me," and she rubbed her thighs, glistening with oil and perspiration, until they quivered. "Would you believe I'm on the go all day and I dance all night and I can't get it off? Everything I eat turns to flesh." She cupped a breast in each hand. "Even my boobs keep growing and I'm thirty-five already." Wonderingly she peered down at the mounds in her hands. She let them go and they bounced.

Maryann gasped and looked away. She had read about

these women, had seen them on television, heard them on talk shows.

("No, it didn't seem unnatural at all in fact the first time —uh—I was with a woman I knew right away that this is how I always felt but was afraid to let myself feel because of society and, you know, being taught that it was—uh—bad and you only had sex with, you know, a man and—uh—anything else was, like you were a pervert and—uh—I don't feel that way anymore. It's, you know, like for the first time I feel as though I have all my shit together and it's—uh—it's dynamite.")

A tear slid down each of Maryann's moist cheeks. Lilyan was baffled and thought, A nut maybe. Could it be something she said? Nah, what'd she say? Nothing. Poor kid, maybe she was sick, maybe she was in deep trouble.

Lilyan sighed and said, "What's the matter, you can tell Lilyan. There's no one here but you and me."

Maryann uttered a single wretched sob. Lilyan watched her awhile and then reached over and took a clean towel from a pile at the end of the bench.

"Here, blow," she said.

Maryann blew and then said a well-bred thank you before closing her eyes again. She had thanked many people that night and willed herself not to cry anymore.

Same to you, sister, Lilyan thought. But she kept an eye on her to make sure she didn't go bananas. The woman had pretty good bone structure. Lilyan could do some job on her face. She probably wasn't a nut. In fact, she looked very refined. So Lilyan said:

"Je suis fatiguée."

With her eyes still closed Maryann said, "Moi aussi."

"Parlez-vous francais?"

"Un peu." Maryann opened her eyes.

Lilyan glanced at her warily. Yeah, well. "You from around here?"

"No."

"Downtown?"

"No."

Lilyan decided she'd try once more, just once more and then the lady could whistle "Hatikvah." "From out of town I'll bet." Maryann nodded. That was it. She knew there was something different about the woman. Lilyan was glad she was right; she liked being right. "Where from?"

Maryann considered the question. "Minneapolis," she said.

"No kidding." Lilyan had never been west of Nyack. "Minneapolis. What are you doing here? Visiting? Gonna stay?"

Maryann consciously clenched her teeth to keep from crying out. "Visiting," she murmured.

"Well, you know what they say, it's a great place to visit but I wouldn't want to live here. But you know that's all wrong." Lilyan leaned forward eagerly. "I think it'd be a terrible place to visit"—she didn't hear Maryann's moan—"but I love living here. I've lived here all my life. We have a place in the eighties. I live with my mother and my brother. My mother's sick, she's got everything, you name it, and we like to keep an eye on her. We don't get in each other's way so I don't mind." She glanced at Maryann. "The place is so big anyway, high ceilings, lots of foyers and stuff. It goes on and on. Besides, my brother keeps crazy hours. He's a writer, graduated summa cum laude from N.Y.U. And I'm out most every night dancing with Lou, my boy friend, at Roseland."

"Where?"

"You don't know Roseland?" Lilyan was genuinely shocked. "Where've you been all your life? See—that's what I mean about New York. You never know a place till you live there. You people come in for a quick visit and take in all the historical places, the Empire State Building, Radio City, Grant's Tomb, and then you go home and figure that's the whole shmeer. You never get the feel of the place. Now when I go abroad," her voice suddenly dropped to what Lilyan called her cultured dulcets, "I try to know what it feels like. I go into the grocery store or a market and buy something and listen to the people talk. Know what I mean? For instance, I just bought a condominium on the Costa Brava. A small place," Lilyan assured Maryann, "one bedroom, just to go over on vacations, me and Lou. But I'll be really living there, getting to know how it feels."

Maryann said she thought it sounded marvelous (it did) and that she envied her (she did). Lilyan looked at her suspiciously; she had to be putting her on, a high-class-looking WASP type like that.

"Who're you kidding? You probably traveled all over the world."

She had always taken for granted that Jack traveled for the company so much he had the right to insist on beaches, golf courses, ski lodges when they were on vacation. And then there was always his mother's place in Michigan.

"Where've you been?" Lilyan challenged.

Maryann was anxious to be honest. "No, really," she said, "We've been to Europe only once, on one of those twenty-one-day charter flights."

"I got it, you're a teacher!" Lilyan's face assumed the ecstasy of a quiz show winner. Maryann denied it. "Then your husband is a teacher!" Maryann said no, he wasn't a teacher either.

Lilyan let a silence come between them; it probably would be exhausting doing this dame's hair. She was ready to stretch out on the bench again but couldn't resist one more attempt.

"So now you're in New York."

"Hmmm."

"With your husband."

"Uh-uh," Maryann shook her head.

Lilyan exploded. "So let me ask you how come you came to this place?" She waved a steamy arm. "Sinus? I mean it's a helluva way to spend a night in New York."

Suddenly and inexplicably Maryann was overwhelmed by the need to confide in this woman who had a boy friend after all. "You won't believe it," she said. Lilyan relaxed; that was more like it. "It all started when I was supposed to come

to New York to spend a few days with my college roommate." (Lilyan had no use for women who had college
roommates in their pasts.) Maryann told her about the boys
being away at camp and Jack at the conference, although she
didn't mention the gold-plated bidet fixtures. "Then my
friend had to go to Italy with her husband so she left the
key to her apartment with the doorman—"

A head above a wrinkled white uniform looked in and said,
"Twunny minutes," and closed the door again.

"What does she mean twunny—twenty minutes?"

"They close at twelve o'clock."

"But I thought this was one of those all-night places!"
Maryann grabbed a towel and covered herself as though
she'd been duped into taking all her clothes off for such a
short time.

"Well, it's not," Lilyan explained. "There used to be
some in Coney Island, maybe there still are, but believe me,
it's too late to go to Coney Island. You're better off going
home to your friend's place."

"That's the point, it's not sinus, I can't get into the apartment. That's what I started to tell you." It didn't matter to
Maryann that she was babbling. "I can't turn the key, it's
the lock or something, it won't open."

"Yeah, well, I see what you mean." Poor thing, Lilyan
thought, she seemed a nice enough person but she was too
tired to get involved with some Mrs. Nutsy from Minneapolis; it seemed so far away. "I guess you can go to a hotel
but it's pretty late. You don't want to look like a jane waiting
for a john. You know what I mean?"

"I think so. What do you mean?"

"A hooker, a prostitute, a whore." Lilyan wanted to avoid
any misunderstanding; she didn't know what they called
them in Minneapolis. "They check into hotels around now,
the big money ones anyway." Maryann was going to cry
again. "You don't know anyone in New York?" Tears were
beginning to dribble down Maryann's cheeks. Lilyan lifted
her eyes to the ceiling and surrendered to someone up there.

"Okay, okay," she said. "Get dressed and you'll come home with me."

"I don't even know you."

"Lilyan with a y Bern. Now you know me."

Maryann adjusted her towel. "Maryann one name Morrison Mansfield."

Wow. So what did the name mean, for Chrissakes? Sally Brown, that was a good shiksa name. Sally Brown meant Sally Brown. Jean Jones was Jean Jones. But Maryann Morrison Mansfield? Those names were adjectives, words in a dictionary.

Lilyan sighed. "You can always go to a hotel in the morning, but tonight you'll come to my place."

"I can't impose on you that way."

"You'd be surprised." She picked up a towel and draped it around Maryann's shoulders. "Don't catch cold," Lilyan said.

7

It is wholly possible, Maryann thought, that she, Maryann, will never be seen again. She knew that was the way these things happened. She had permitted herself (no kicking, protesting, scratching, screaming, "Help help police I'm being kidnapped") to enter a taxi while, ludicrous under the circumstances, Lilyan carried her hand luggage. She drew back into the dark far corner of the seat but then edged a little toward the center so that the driver could see her in his rear-view mirror in case he ever had to identify a photograph of her.

She should have passed a note to the girl at the front desk of the health spa:

> I am being kidnapped. Please
> call my husband who won't be there
> in Chagrin Falls.

Instead she gave the girl one of her twenty-dollar bills and not only waited for the change but waited for Lilyan.

The girl, a round, brown-eyed Puerto Rican, said to Lilyan with a suspicious familiarity, "Goin' hon now?" Maryann thought it was heavy with innuendo, a veiled and ominous message. They were part of a syndicate. Maryann had heard about that sort of thing. White slavers. Looking for nubile forty-year-olds. "Maybe I'll see ya Monthay. I gotta do son'ing abot my culla."

Lilyan reached over the desk and flipped back a strand of the girl's hair. "You could use it," she said. "Come over anytime, I'll squeeze you in."

That was for her benefit, Maryann thought, a ruse of respectability, of ordinariness, to lull her suspicions.

When Lilyan stepped out into the street to get the cab, Maryann could see herself in her mind, breaking away from the curb and running down the street, panting, while Lilyan (big, beefy Lilyan) overcomes her in three big loping strides and knocks her to the ground.

"Oh no you don't, pigeon."

And a dark and menacing figure emerges from a hidden doorway saying doomfully: "Good thing you didn't let her get away, the boss wouldn't have liked it."

Or, breaking away from the curb and running down the street, panting, while Lilyan (big, beefy Lilyan) whips out a gun, a shot rings out and a bullet neatly pierces Maryann's aorta. (Does Lilyan run off or go back into the Sauna, faking fear, reporting a mysterious shot that killed her companion whom she never laid eyes on before that evening so why, Officer, would she even want to kill her?)

Maryann stepped meekly into the taxi.

They were heading uptown, Maryann knew; she didn't actually hear the exact address, 300 something Eighty-third Street.

"It's not far, honey. What we need is a little tea and brandy and bed. Maybe I'll skip the tea."

The truth was that Maryann saw the immediate future that way too, yet still dabbled with the possibility that this was the end, the way fate unfolded, seemingly innocently but undoubtedly by mysterious design. God knows she hoped not. She was now weary and wanted to believe this warm-hearted woman was offering her shelter for the night and a cup of coffee in the morning, like the vagrant she was. Maryann's eyelids quivered in an attempt to stay open. She had been up since five that morning (already yesterday) helping Jack pack bathing suits (2); tennis whites (3); golf shoes (2); dinner jacket (1); evening shirt with pink ruffle trim (1); cufflinks (2); cummerbund (1); for his business seminar.

Lilyan wouldn't let Maryann pay the taxi fare, skittering up the front steps saying that it was "her ride." That left

Maryann at the bottom of the stoop, clutching her money and gazing up at the building where Lilyan lived. It was a dismal gray five-story structure with ornate gargoyles snuggled between fluted bas-relief. Over the front door, the words "BICKFORD ARMS" were chiseled into the keystone. The large window on the right side of the entrance was protected by metal bars. A sign in the left bottom corner said "NOTARY" and in the other corner, "ALTERATIONS." A cat sat among some plants on the windowsill and peered through the leaves.

Never seen again, not by Jack or John or Tommy or her mother or her brother or Mary Anne at Pick-N-Pay. Forget the piece of luggage. Run for your life, she urged herself once more but Lilyan's eager face turned and smiled at her as she opened the front door.

Well, she wrote her own epitaph:

> Here lies Maryann Morrison Mansfield,
> Too embarrassed to save herself.
> In case she was wrong
> She didn't want to appear
> Ridiculous
> To strangers.

If she ever saw Jack again, how could she explain to him that she had gone home with a total stranger? In New York. This was exactly the kind of thing she always warned them about. Jack and the kids. "You must never go down to the end of the town if you don't go down with me."

(She could have evoked a line from Milton, "And found no end, in wand'ring mazes lost . . ." something, something, but A. A. Milne best described her philosophy.)

Lilyan opened the vestibule door with a key. "One flight up," she said, an apology. Suddenly she was shy. "Sorry, these old tenements don't have elevators."

A strange, sharp odor dominated the hallway. It was tangy, decidedly unpleasant, and seemed to be leavened into the faded brown walls. A staircase went up the left side wall; on the right was a door and deep into the hallway, hidden in darkness, was another door.

The stairs creaked as first Lilyan and then Maryann ascended. Suddenly Maryann stopped halfway up. She remembered there was a mother and a brother at the top of the stairs behind the closed door. A crazy old woman and a deranged man. (This was a touch of Dashiell Hammett.) An older man, a cracked soul whose unbalanced mind wallowed in perversions. Or was it a younger brother, queer, unhinged, witless, whose sadistic evils amused the cackling crone? They would hide her in a closet and practice their depravities on her until she became a mindless vegetable, their very own thing. At first Jack would search for her and her heart ached for Jack searching vainly. She saw him in slow motion lifting one leg and then the other as though stuck in molasses. He'd trace her to Ginny's building.

"Idunno," the doorman would say. "Some dame from Topeka was here. But she left her bags." Aha! Saved! Jack would recognize her luggage. "The last I saw she was heading for Lexington Avenue going to the Waldorf."

But they never heard of her at the Waldorf and how would Jack know she got off at Fifty-sixth Street? Her mind simply couldn't accept that possibility. Somehow through uncanny superhuman deductions he would trace her to the health spa. The girl would tell him that she was last seen with Lilyan Byrne. No, that was wrong; the girl wouldn't tell: she was part of the mob. Maybe they weren't crazy, maybe they were a mob—Ma Byrne's Gang. They'd keep her prisoner once she knew their hideout.

"What the hellaya bring her here for," slap, slap, Lilyan clutches her bleeding mouth. "Now she knows where we are, she'll blow the whistle. We'll have to keep her here indefinitely."

Ma Byrne wouldn't use the word indefinitely. Maryann searched her brain but couldn't come up with a synonym. Anyway, they'd have to keep her there. And, yes, the allotted seven years later she would be declared dead and Jack would marry again; he should marry again. (Or did she want him to search the world over in desert tents, seraglios, grim stone mansions in the North Country of England?) But meanwhile, Maryann would be dead without having left any letters or instructions in secret drawers telling the boys about life, values, hopes, dreams, and to go to the dentist twice a year; it was important to keep one's own teeth. If she had known, she would have written a letter to Jack's new wife too. Telling her, pleading with her, to love them all, love them all.

(What an awful conceit, this interfering manipulation of one's will after death, Maryann suddenly thought with sensible distaste. But then, there is no question that the core of life also is one's ego. Isn't that right, Mrs. Dinosaur?)

"Uhhh," Lilyan said and stopped on the top step.

"Grggrg," Maryann replied.

"You say something?"

"No, no!"

"Oh. Well," Lilyan felt awkward, "listen. Uh, you remember I said that I—you recall, you know, about that condominium on the Costa Brava?"

"Yes?"

"I don't have one."

"Oh."

Lilyan peered down at Maryann. "Castles in Spain, right?"

"Sure," Maryann said kindly. "At least you dream."

Lilyan grinned at her and approached the door at the top of the landing, but then she turned to Maryann again, frowning. "The apartment. It's a—"

"Oh, look," Maryann said gently, "I'm sure I'm putting you to a great deal of trouble. Why don't I just call a hotel from your place?"

"I wouldn't hear of it. Don't get me wrong, we always have an extra bed." Lilyan inserted the key in the door lock.

"Hey! I don't come from Minneapolis." Maryann's offer was generous.

"No kidding, where are you from?"

"Chagrin Falls."

"Where the hell is that?"

"Ohio. Near Cleveland."

Lilyan considered it for a moment. Then she shrugged. "I liked Minneapolis, it has a better beat. You can dance to it."

MINN-e-a-po-lis -a- MINN-e-a-po-lis -a- MINN—

8

The door flew open and a small woman, looking like an untied bundle, stood on the threshold. She wore a loosely fitted print cotton dress, its two front pockets protuberant, lumpy with things. Her skinny legs could not quite fill out her stockings and they stood away from the flesh as though they had a life of their own; the cuffs of white socks emerged from the soft bedroom slippers. On her head was a blue-and-red woolen ski hat out of which escaped wisps of coarse bleached blond hair. A string of white plastic beads around her neck and a single pink hair roller on her forehead were her only ornaments. She seemed in harmony with the throb of rock music that came from another place.

"Thank God you're home, Lillie, any minute I would have called the police. God bless Him, we should only know from good things." She looked beyond Lilyan and saw a woman who seemed to be loitering in the doorway. "Should I know her, Lillie?"

"No, Ma."

"You brought her?"

"Yes, Ma."

"So come in, lady, come in." The woman waved hospitably with an aerosol can of Raid cockroach spray. Maryann watched her double-lock the door and put on a latch chain.

Lilyan and her mother propelled Maryann into a small living room that bulged with large upholstered furniture and oversized lamps festooned in plastic coverlets. Low tables were layered with small glass swans, tiny china figurines, framed snapshots and large posed pictures of wedding parties and gala celebrants, souvenirs from Florida and the Stork Club, a miniature Model T Ford and a miniature cannon that later proved to be cigarette lighters, and a bowl of goldfish. On the walls were two mirrors with gilt frames, three calendars and prints of Van Goghs, Renoirs and Gauguins in plastic shadow boxes. (They hung at random. In fact, wherever there had been a previous nail.)

"Sit down," the mother urged Maryann amiably, prodding her into a chair. "Offer your friend a drink, Lilyan, it's only one in the morning."

Lilyan coaxed Maryann up again and said, "C'mon into the kitchen, don't be such a stranger. She's staying overnight, Ma."

"That's different," the mother said, "then I'll give you something to eat."

There was neither a hall nor a foyer between the rooms and the two women as escorts almost lifted Maryann across the threshold into the kitchen.

"Lillie darling, who is she?" the mother asked as though Maryann wasn't wedged between them. If she weren't so tired and bewildered, Maryann would have slipped out and escaped into the New York summer night, gladly leaving her bag behind.

"Say hello to Eddie. Eddie, this is my friend Maryann, I met her in the steam room. She's from Cleveland and she didn't have a place to stay"—Maryann winced—"so I told her to stay with us. Right?" Lilyan's head then disappeared into the refrigerator.

"Absolutely right," the mother said. It was clearly the appropriate decision. She considered her children her emissaries in the world, reflecting her hospitality, spirit and good will.

The rock music blared from a small radio on a shelf over an old two-legged porcelain sink; a portable television set was propped on a kitchen chair. On the screen William Powell was stirring a martini and Myrna Loy played with the dog, Asta. At the gold-flecked formica table a stocky, muscular man with dark curly hair hunched over a bowl of cornflakes, milk and sliced bananas, as though protecting it from some other glutton. His eyes flickered intently from the television screen to the Dick Tracy comic strip in the *Daily News* that was propped against a vase of plastic roses. His spoon dipped regularly, with a faithful rhythm, into the bowl and to his mouth. Maryann often experienced déjà vu but this was not one of those times. To her knowledge, she had never before known this moment.

"Eddie!" Lilyan yelled. "Stand up for Chrissakes, there's a lady in the room."

"Blow it," he said, his mouth full, and shouting at William Powell, "I love it!" When he threw his body back in the chair in ecstasy he saw Maryann.

"Don't say I didn't warn you. I warned him, didn't I, Ma?" What a laugh on Eddie; wait till she told them at the shop how she faked him out.

I'll kill her for this, Eddie thought, pushing his chair back finally, standing and grinning, putting both hands on his chest and rubbing his undershirt.

"Okay, so meet my new friend Maryann. You'll have to excuse my brother," Lilyan said, "no manners."

"How do you do?" Maryann said from a great distance.

Eddie believed in timing and he knew it was too late to say pleased to meet you. He nodded with what he hoped was the right amount of perfunctoriness, indifference and charm. Lil brought them all home, a sick dog she had diagnosed, a scabrous cat evicted from the fish market, a hamster whose owner was going to a Fresh Air Camp for two weeks, plants to water while a customer was at Grossinger's in the Catskills. But never anything like this. Blond and green-eyed, not his idea of a beauty but not bad either. He knew the type. He picked them up at the airport and brought them to small hotels or some East Side address. The kind of woman he'd muse about for a few minutes after he'd drop her off: what kind of lay she was; do it but don't touch me while you're doing it. Sometimes they invited him up.

Sometimes he accepted. What the hell was she doing in his kitchen?

"You weren't listening. Maryann is in New York for a few days from—where?"

"Chagrin Falls."

"Yeah, anyway, she couldn't get into her friend's apartment. She lost the key."

"It didn't work. I couldn't—"

"Right, something. So here she is." Lilyan removed things from the refrigerator: a gallon carton of milk, two covered Tupperware containers, a half-finished chocolate layer cake, a jug of orange juice, a bottle of cream soda, a bowl of fruit.

"Excuse my guinea smoking jacket. I'll go put something on." He managed to shuffle and swagger at the same time. He knew it was one of his better imitations of Marlon Brando.

"Maybe we should have called and warned your family," Maryann said. "I don't think your brother is too happy about me." She wasn't too happy about him either.

"Tough," Lilyan said, her voice muffled by chocolate cake hastily devoured, "he's not the only one who lives here." She rearranged the disarray on the table to make room for the food, opened one of the containers, and dipped a finger in the congealed gravy. "Pot roast, delicious, want some? My mother's a terrific cook."

"Please, I don't want to trouble you. I'm not very hungry," Maryann said, famished.

The mother placed a plate in front of Maryann; it had a faded border of forget-me-nots. "It was from my good set, there's only two plates and a cup left but I hate to throw them out." Then she picked a cherry out of the fruit bowl and dropped the stem into one of her pockets. "Open," she commanded and put the cherry into Maryann's mouth. Cherry juice dribbled down Maryann's chin. "See, what did I tell you? God bless nature. I know my cherries," she said. And then, "I'll kill it!" and Maryann swallowed the pit.

The woman lunged for the can of Raid and violently sprayed a cockroach ambling across the wall above the sink. "They should all rot in hell, the poor things," she said, prowling the kitchen. "Did you know it's a proven fact that there are more cockroaches in the world than people? A house down the block, they wanted to evict everyone so they could tear down the building and put up a fancy high rise. But they couldn't get the people out so you know what they did? I'll tell you. They fired the exterminator. You get the significance? In one week that building was overrun by cockroaches and the people had to escape like refugees. If our landlord, that son of a bitch momser, not that he's such a terrible person, ever tried it on us I'd see him in his grave with the cockroaches together." She placed the can of Raid on the sink, wiped her hands on her dress and smiled benignly at Maryann. "Eat, don't be bashful, Miriam." She sat down at the table and pushed the carton of milk aside, the better to see her guest.

"Maryann, Ma."

"Marion? Probably your mother was a Marion Davies fan."

"It's Mary and Ann together." Maryann's smile was strained. "One name."

"You're sure it's not Marion for Marion Davies?"

"I was named for my grandmothers."

"They died so young?" She was prepared to grieve.

"No, no! In fact, they both died recently, fairly old."

She was unconvinced. "My own kids were named for Lilyan Tashman and Edmund Lowe. You know them? I didn't think so. They were before your time. Someday I'll tell you about them. Personally, my name was Fanny but I changed it to Fay. For Fay Wray. As soon as I laid eyes on that woman I knew she had my name. Did you ever see her in the movies? She was simply a little doll. He really loved her a lot, that King Kong. It was a sad picture. I didn't have the heart to see it when they made it again. He could crush her like a *vonce* but he loved her. I'll tell you something, that was the way I used to feel about their father, my husband, he should rest in peace."

"Don't get her started on that."

"Why not? Mine was a love story too. Love and hate, that's a love story." Suddenly Fay felt cranky; it happened often lately. For no reason, she would feel blue. She'd feel her body ache and her memories irritate. Maybe she had cancer of the spleen. "Where's Eddie? Go see what's taking him so long."

"He's alive, he's alive," Lilyan muttered going down the dark corridor. It seemed as though she spent most of her life looking to see if Eddie was alive.

"I know I'm keeping you up, Mrs. Byrne. Why don't you go to sleep? I'll call a hotel and I thank you for being so kind."

"Fay Bern sleep at night? You're in the wrong pew. Oh, I beg your pardon, no offense intended. You're not going to a hotel. Take a few more bites, you hardly touched a thing."

"I've eaten more tonight than I did all day."

"I guess you chew so refined I hardly know you're eating. Chew like you enjoy."

"I am enjoying," Maryann said, surprised that she really meant it. She would have to sneak away when no one was looking and later ask sweet Jesus to forgive her.

"I set a good table," Fay agreed, waving her hand vaguely over the apparition of food, containers, dishes. "Maryann what?"

"What?"

"What's your last name?"

"Oh—Mansfield."

Fay was overcome with emotion; she forgot her momentary depression. "That's beautiful. What was it before?"

"Before I was married?"

"You mean that's your real name, Maryann Mansfield? Did you hear that, Lillie?" she bawled. "Sweetheart, with a name like that you could have been a movie star. You're a good-looking person, too. Such a waste."

"I like your name too, Mrs. Byrne." ("Call me Fay.")
"That's a Kildare name, Byrne. My father had cousins in
Kildare. His grandfather was the only one of three brothers
who came to the United States around the eighteen sixties.
I've always regretted not knowing more about them. I'd like
to go to Ireland some day and look them up."

Lilyan returned wearing a faded Japanese kimono. She
sat down at the table and began to roll her hair around large
blue curlers. Her laughter was a whinny: "Honey, it's not
Byrne from Kildare. It's Bern from Minsk. It used to be
Bernstein. Look at her, she's blushing."

"The descendants of Chekhov's bourgeois intelligentsia,
victims of pogroms and other passions." Eddie was standing
in the doorway of the kitchen, his aftershave lotion mingled
with the lingering acridity of Raid. He wore clean chinos
and a LaCoste tennis shirt (Maryann didn't believe he played
tennis), and his hair was brushed and damp from the shower.

"Don't worry," Fay said, patting Maryann's hand, "we eat
everything."

"Chekhov, my ass. My brother suffers from delusions. Our
grandfather had a pushcart on Essex and Hester Streets."

"But he kept the collected works of de Maupassant under
the BVDs."

"They were for sale."

"Mr. Macy started out life with a pushcart, Mr. Gimbel
started out life with a pushcart. But Grandpa's pushcart
helped like dead potatoes. Do you know that expression?"
she asked Maryann.

"She wouldn't know, Ma," Eddie grinned.

Fay shrugged. "She might." After all, how should she know
what the goyim in Ohio knew? She sighed, glancing at Eddie.
Suddenly for no reason at all her eyes were warm with joyous
tears.

"Look at you," she said, "a Bruce Cabot, an Errol Flynn,
an Alan Jones, a Cary Grant."

He got all spiffied up for the shiksa at two in the morning.

Chinos that she had ironed that day for the weekend, now he wouldn't wear them again; tomorrow he'll take a clean pair of pants.

Fay looked at Maryann: she wasn't even his type. Fay couldn't count how many women Eddie had known through the years and three times he was engaged. Once to a little nothing from Staten Island. Fay wouldn't even let her in the house. Eddie was a kid, he just started college and he used to come home wild after a night of feeling her up in his car outside her house. What's-her-name; Fay refused to remember her name. Her father wanted Eddie to go into his business, he was a butcher. Then he was engaged to Miss Fancy Shmancy from West End Avenue. She was studying to be a speech therapist and had long black hair and two big brown eyes. Her father was a doctor; very rich. Fay could have managed with her, Sandra. At least the wedding invitation would have read Dr. and Mrs. Norman Pitkin announce the marriage of their daughter Sandra Joy to Mr. Edmund Bern and Fay would have walked down the aisle with her son in the Terrace Room of the Plaza. In the end, that was the only thing Fay regretted, the loss of that particular moment and memory. But what happened was that everything had to match with Sandra Joy; her pocketbook, her shoes, her dress, her handkerchief, her compact inside her pocketbook. Even her titties matched. Fay saw them once when Sandra slept over. Most women, one side was a little different than the other, but not by Sandra. Hers were a perfect match.

Then a few months before the wedding, in the morning while he was eating cornflakes, Eddie said: "God, I can't do it!"

"Stop yelling at Him!"

"I can't and I won't!"

Fay didn't have to ask what he couldn't and wouldn't. She knew. He couldn't marry a girl who had to have everything match. At least that's what he said was the reason. Fay wasn't surprised. Maybe if they had just gone off and gotten married quietly it would have been all right. But the bridesmaids' hats had to match the ruffles on the ushers' shirts and the matchbooks had to match the trimming on the tablecloths and the icing on the cake had to match Sandra's underwear. You needed months, years, to match things just right.

Take Eddie; he was a different type altogether. In the days when Fay was feeling good and still going outside, he'd park the cab somewhere (he always made extra money with cabs, even when he was going to college) and they'd go over to Broadway and mix with the crowds at intermission. Then they'd sneak in and see the last act. One season they saw ten second acts and two third acts and it was okay with Eddie, if you get the significance. A person with that temperament had to say goodbye to Sandra Joy.

But the last time was a sad business. He had no luck, her Eddie. (A million times she asked herself: did she do that to him when she named him for Edmund Lowe, who was still alive at the time?) Fay would never forget her. Judy. She had something special. A sweetness. A beautiful person. Even Lillie liked her. She worked in an office and then went back to school to be a social worker. Then she got sick; very sick. It was a blood sickness, God forbid, would you believe a young girl like that, twenty-six. As soon as she found out, Judy wouldn't see Eddie anymore. She gave him back the ring, a 1.6 carat with two baguettes on each side in a Tiffany setting. Fay's brother-in-law Murray got it for Eddie wholesale from a jeweler friend of his downtown on Maiden Lane. Never, never, never had she seen Eddie cry like he cried. Days and nights he cried and then he used to call Judy's house and her mother cried. She won't talk to you Eddie, she's killing me, the poor woman said. Eddie used to sit in the lobby of Judy's building, a big apartment house on Grand Army Plaza in Brooklyn, waiting to see her parents, her brother, a friend, anyone who knew her. He said he'd marry her anyway, he didn't care if he had to carry her from the bed to the toilet, he would marry her. Even Fay didn't have the heart to say no. By the time she died—it wasn't too long, only months—Eddie couldn't cry anymore. He went to the funeral and then he sat shiva with the family. He used to visit her parents every night like he was the son-in-law, a widower. Every night, then three times a week, then once a week, then only occasionally. It was now a few years since he saw them. But he wrote a story about Judy and it was published in a magazine, *Atlantic Monthly,* which although people said it was a very fine magazine Fay wasn't personally too familiar with it. He called it "The Bride." It was the first time he had a story published. Fay could cry right now just thinking about it. They should all live and be well and only have good luck. God should only bless them. From her mouth to His ears.

Fay didn't feel so good suddenly.

"Your hair is wet. You'll catch a cold in a draft," she said to Eddie.

He grabbed her ski cap off her head and set it on his head. "You don't need your hat. We're all home now."

Fay squealed girlishly, "Give it back to me, my hair's a mess."

"I want to hear you tell Maryann why you wear a hat in the house and then I'll give it back to you."

"It's no big mystery," she said, indignant. "I'm not ashamed. When I look out the window the least little wind gives me an earache," she told Maryann. She settled the woolen hat carefully, tucking in all loose hair. "Listen, Mr. Smartass, if it wasn't for your mother looking up and down the block from the window you might be dead now, God forbid, I'll bite my tongue. I must have saved your life I don't know how many times. New York is a wonderful town but it's not always a safe place, Marion. You heard about it in Cleveland, I'm sure the whole world knows by now. Lillie comes home late from the shop or the sauna or from dancing at Roseland and sometimes Lou can't bring her. Eddie, if he has a date or if he's on the night shift with the cab, comes God knows how late. Take tonight," Fay said. Eddie was supposed to come home at midnight and a quarter of one he wasn't home yet. How long does it take to walk home from the garage, five blocks away? "I was ready to fall out the window."

"Every block is a memory. Seventy-eighth Street a girl I used to know, Eightieth Street a guy I owe money to. My route is devious."

Muggers could come out of nowhere and hit him on the head, Fay told Maryann, and leave him for dead in the gutter. She could be in the house only a short distance away humming and singing and not know that her only son was lying there dying, bleeding to death, maybe going into a coma never to speak to her again, she said. "I figure if I look out the window I could help him, scream for the police, do something. He, big shot, he'd like me to be asleep in my bed while he's laying in the gutter. Do you get my meaning?"

Maryann stared at the woolen ski cap, stricken, and murmured, "Actually"—she wouldn't look at Eddie—"I do."

"I had a feeling in my heart that you would, darling! Just for that I'll tell your fortune." Fay pulled out a pack of cards from a pocket, shuffled them expertly and then turned them up singly until she came to the Queen of Hearts. "That's you," she said to Maryann and placed it facedown on the table. "Confidentially, I believe in fate, don't you?" she said. She dealt four cards, facedown, side by side, and continued until she had five piles of cards. She then turned up the top card of each stack. A Jack of Hearts topped the stack with the Queen of Hearts at the bottom. Fay seemed disappointed. "A blondish man, maybe brown hair, is in your life." (Certainly it wasn't Eddie. Eddie was the King of Spades.) "Do you know him?"

"Would you believe her husband, Ma?" Eddie said from the pages of the *News.*

"You have a husband, Marion?"

"She's wearing a wedding ring," Lilyan said.

"That doesn't mean anything these days. It could be a friendship ring made out of elephant hair."

"Where did you say he was?" Lilyan asked through chocolate crumbs.

Suddenly Jack was in the room. Maryann hadn't thought of him since she walked in the door. That realization alone was a blow. "He's at a business seminar," she said and then quickly clamped her teeth to imprison her tongue. There would not be one word about tennis courts, Olympic-sized pools and golden faucets or who else was at the conference.

Fay looked at her shrewdly and started to say something but changed her mind. "That's nice," she said. She gathered the cards impatiently; the Jack of Hearts was not her favorite card. "Tomorrow I'll do it right. Come, Lillie, we'll fix the bed." Not another word about hotels or living room sofas and it wasn't any trouble at all.

Maryann rose politely, a little confused by the conversation that had swirled around her, everyone answering for her. "Thank you, Fay, I'm sure I'm a bother to you." Fay hugged her, startling Maryann, who remembered her relatives' fluttering butterfly intimacies. "You're really very kind," she said, submitting to the embrace, her eyes following two cockroaches airily taking a walk on thready legs across the wall above the refrigerator.

"What kind, what bother? New Yorkers are known for our hospitality. My casa is your casa," Fay said coyly, "it's like a party. You sit with Eddie a little, he's a very intellectual person."

From somewhere down the hall they could hear Fay singing about some enchanted evening.

Eddie said he would help Maryann in the morning, drive her to the apartment and see what he could do about the lock, certainly he could get her bags to a hotel. She said that was very nice of him but she hated to trouble him in any way and she would leave quite early in the morning. He said no, it was perfectly all right, he had to take the cab out for a few hours. She said something about wasn't he a writer and that seemed to be the wrong thing to say.

"I drive a cab," he said abruptly. (Fuck off, lady, I'm not going to be a writer for you. This is Fanny Bernstein's house where the cockroaches are running like the Bulls of Pamplona. I drive a cab and I need Mrs. Mansfield like I need another set of balls.)

Fay called from the back of the apartment. "Eddie? Maryann?"

"We're alive, we're alive," Eddie said irritably and turned up the television sound.

Maryann stood up. He was a clod.

William Powell fixed another drink. Asta barked.

9

Lilyan's room was small and dark; the only window looked out on a lightless shaft, its view protected from sight by a dusty venetian blind and a window fan. Clothes on hangers hung from hooks on the wall; brassieres and stockings were piled carelessly on a chair; magazines lay in a heap on the floor near the bed, and on the dresser was a jumble of makeup in elaborate bottles, perfumes, lipsticks, rouges, a plastic tree dangling earrings and necklaces, a faceless wooden dummy wearing a long wavy black wig. In a small clear box, eyelashes that looked as though they were from a decapitated llama viewed the confusion with cool detachment. Pictures on the wall were of Lilyan and a man in each other's arms (she wearing taffeta and chiffon gowns and he in a tuxedo) frozen in various dance positions.

"Pas de deux," said Lilyan, her large body executing a sweetly graceful pirouette.

There wasn't much space between Lilyan's bed and a narrow cot they had opened up for Maryann. Maryann was about to get into bed when she remembered her decongestion pill. Surreptitiously she took one out of the bottle in her handbag and swallowed it. It stuck to her throat and felt bitter and grainy but she didn't permit herself the long walk down the corridor for a drink of water.

Fay looked in. "Good night, Marion Davies," she said, a coquette, "good night, Lilyan Tashman."

"Go to bed, Fay Wray," Lilyan sighed.

Lilyan's body was grateful for the cool sheets; she had eaten too much again. Tomorrow just water, she swore on her life. "Let's sleep late tomorrow, and maybe we'll go over to Roseland in the afternoon," she said cozily to Maryann. "I'll call Lou and we'll get Eddie to come too. I'll teach you to mambo. You'll really like Lou. He's basically a very swell guy. Very romantic. He says things like 'We'll dance together through life under the stars' or 'We'll always hear music when we're together.' I could die. Don't get me wrong, it's really adorable, but sometimes I feel like laughing. Once I couldn't help it and I started laughing and he says to me why are you crying. And it was true, I was crying." She laughed heartily in huge gulps. Before she fell asleep she thought, Look at that, after all these years she had a roommate.

Maryann decided it wasn't the right time to explain that she would be leaving in the morning, and Lilyan fell into a rhythmic snoring almost immediately. She might leave her some of her decongestion pills before she went.

She lay quietly, waiting for sleep, apprehensive in the alien setting. Bern, Byrne: she could feel herself blushing again. The sheets, the light blanket, the walls, smelled differently than anything she had known. (Some of it was Raid, she knew; that's what that odor was in the downstairs hallway, a stale history of Raid.) But besides the Raid, other people's houses smelled differently as though they exuded not only the odor of favorite foods or the type of detergents used, but more specifically, the chemicals of the bodies that lived in the house. It occurred to her that she was a woman approaching forty and had never before seen a cockroach. Giant ants, termites, bees, wasps, ladybugs. No cockroaches. She shivered, hoping they weren't crawling all around her.

There was a thud against the wall and Maryann's heart lurched. It was from Eddie's room; his bed must be against the same wall as Maryann's. She moved restlessly, embarrassed by the intimate proximity.

That night she chased vivid, kinetic pictures through a fitful dream (which she promptly forgot in the morning):

A hairy ape stood on the roof of her house. He had an

erection. Maryann was on the lawn shouting up to it to come down before Jack got home. Then, suddenly, she was in her kitchen and it was Tommy standing on the counter trying to reach the top shelf of the cupboard. What are you looking for? she asked him and Tommy answered with Eddie's voice: Dope, do I know what I'm looking for?

Eddie groaned noisily. He couldn't sleep. He tortured himself by going over his conversation with Maryann. He'll help her get her bags to a hotel. Oh no, it's no trouble at all. Blah blah blah. Where was his Noel Coward wit, his Mel Brooks zaniness, the depth and worldliness of Woody Allen's absurd view of life? He considered knocking on the door with his "It's the rapist, ma'am, where shall I put it?" line, but Lilyan would kill him.

Why did she bring her home? Lilyan was a pain in the ass. Always was. When he was a kid and they went to Brighton Beach, Fay would send Lilyan to the locker to see if he was alive. He'd be jerking off among the women's underwear. "What're you doing in there," she'd scream, banging on the door, "jerking off?" The best he could do was wait in the cabana for his hard on to go soft. That was Lil for you.

In the end what bothered him most was wasting his good chinos for one lousy hour with a tightass married shiksa. It was a crazy story about the key. She might be some new kind of hustler in town for all he knew; you never can tell. But now his chinos were wrinkled and he liked clean, fresh clothes on Saturday morning.

Saturdays he liked to feel new, ready for anything.

SATURDAY

10

In the morning Maryann's first sensation was that of being nestled in a confusion of litter. Even Lilyan in the next bed was a lump, a pile of dispossessed bedding. Three baby blue curlers emerged from the edge of the blanket and the rest of her hair flopped about as though she shared the pillow with an unkempt cocker spaniel. She also knew an unfamiliar feeling of triumph and might have permitted herself a fond, self-indulgent chuckle—just a small ha ha—if she hadn't been afraid of awakening Lilyan. Among strangers in an unfamiliar place and she had survived to see the sun rise.

New York was well, she was alive and cockroaches were living in Fay Bern's apartment. She was glad. What right had she, at her age, never to have seen a cockroach?

This was how Jack managed it. He too came home from his many trips, still a living, breathing, loving human life. It always seemed somewhat magical to her, considering the strangers he encountered, the countless takeoffs and landings, the isolated roads he traveled in rented cars, the distant cities he went to. (The women he met?) Take Dallas or Seattle for instance, cities Maryann had never been to. Because she had never been there she viewed them as terra incognita, inhabited by uncivilized tribes of mysterious origin and fathomed for the first time by the brave and/but foolish explorer Jack Mansfield. Occasionally, she would reveal this timorousness to Jack although tidying up the fears a little to make them seem more reasonable. But Jack nailed them like delicate specimens to examine critically. She knew her anxieties were a burden to Jack, so she would hurry to say, "You're silly to take me seriously. You know

I'm only joking." "No you're not," he would answer wisely.

Jack too awakened in other rooms. But at that moment she didn't want to think about it. After all, she didn't know anything for a fact. For the first time that she could recall she didn't want to think about Jack at all. She didn't want him there with her in Lilyan's room. Nor did she want to see the whole thing through his eyes.

How would he see it? (And there she was, seeing it through Jack's eyes.) She made a mental list:

1) insulted by a cab driver,
2) no place to stay,
3) left her baggage with a man she didn't know,
4) owed him $1.10 besides,
5) took five cents from a poor working woman she'd never see again,
6) went home with person unknown (unknown: i.e., Jewish, mysterious, smart, pushy).

And there she was in a strange bed among these very strange strangers. But even that wasn't the point. The point was that what seemed totally unexplainable could be easily explained. How could she explain that to Jack?

She did it; she was seeing it all through his eyes. Maryann's initial exhilaration was replaced by exhaustion brought on by depression.

She knew what she would do. In the morning light it was hardly a mystery and she was in no need of rescue. She would tiptoe out, go to Ginny's for her bags and take a cab to the airport. Once home she would rearrange the drawers and clean out the boys' closets and have a few days to think up a good story to tell Jack. (Certainly not the truth. He would never cease to tease her about it and demand that she laugh at herself too. At the moment Maryann didn't see herself laughing at herself for the rest of her life.)

She would leave a nice note for the Berns, send them a gift once she got home (but without a return address) and if in future years she felt guilty about sneaking out, she would worry about it then.

Feeling hot, sticky, furious with herself, she put on her clothes and walked carefully down the corridor, every creak of the old floorboards a threat. In the bathroom she locked the door and undressed again. She considered taking a shower but decided the noise would cut off her escape. Instead Maryann tried to wash her body at the sink but the ancient hot-water pipes let out a great and piercing screech. She hurriedly turned down the faucet to a trickle, dabbed at her body futilely and blotted herself with toilet paper. For façade, a generous splash of cologne, more eye makeup than usual, a heavier brush of lipstick. She looked at herself in the mirror and decided she could pass for respectable on the flight home.

With her case and handbag she moved stealthily to the kitchen to scribble a few words of gratitude and place them where they would be seen.

"Mimi darling—one—you're up already—two—God bless— three—why didn't you sleep some more—four—it's early—five —" Fay was filling an electric coffeepot and smiled at Maryann with her full set of capped teeth. She wasn't wearing her ski hat since both Lilyan and Eddie were safely in bed, and her blond, straw-bleached hair was placed slyly over bald spots.

"Why are you up? You got to bed late too."

"I'm like an owl, I sleep during the day. At night my heart beats too fast, my legs hurt something awful. I lay there and listen to my body and I get scared of what I hear. We need milk, Mimi. Eddie drank it all last night. Wait, I'll ask Eddie for some money and you'll go to the store for me."

"Don't, please, I—"

But Fay had slipped into Eddie's room and deftly removed a five-dollar bill from his wallet without awakening him.

"He was only too happy," she said when she returned. "Right on the corner you'll find a grocery store."

She took Maryann's luggage out of her hand saying that no one left Fay Bern's house in the morning without breakfast. "Get rolls too."

(When Maryann was on the street, Fay's head appeared at the window. "Don't forget the *Times* for Eddie," she yelled.)

Lilyan wore her limp kimono and the halo of baby blue curlers. She accepted Maryann's presence cheerfully although Fay seemed anxious. She wanted "everything should be nice," Fay told Lilyan. She set the kitchen table with place mats and arranged a paper napkin in each coffee cup hoping it looked like a flower just bloomed, and with the obsequiousness of a headwaiter she asked: "Fried, poached or scrambled?"

Eddie was churlish. He was certain the day was destined to be lousy. He had faced and was defeated by the insurmountable problem: should he wear the same chinos and shirt as the night before? He put them on, took them off and knew it was a masochistic urge that made him put them on again. All in all he sensed bad vibes. The rhythm of the household, its normal beat, its basic timing, was off, like a movie out of sync. He hardly trusted his lips to move with the sound of his voice. (Maybe he could pursue that idea for a story.)

Years later, Maryann conjured up the morning as a wild and crazy hovering of time seen through a slightly cracked kaleidoscope. Fragmented color and motion but with sound effects. There was crunching, chewing, the clatter of forks and knives, the rattling of cups and plates, as accompaniment for swirling eggy yellow and white contrasts, deep browns and tans of coffee, rolls and toast, the dense white of milk and cream cheese, a piquant glimpse of strawberry jam. The room was becoming soft and resilient with summer heat. Emergency sirens clamored for space. Trucks and buses changed gears on the street below, perpetually being urged up an imperceptible incline.

Through it all the Berns ate with the unconcerned ease of picnickers in a still meadow. Even Maryann, wondering how she could get away without insulting them, managed to eat two scrambled eggs, two rolls with substantial dabs of butter and jam and several gratifying swallows of hot coffee.

There was conversation.

E: [*Lifting the blooming napkin out of his coffee cup*] Is this a fucking catered affair or something?

M: [*shocked murmur*] I think it's sweet.

Fay sighs.

L: Eddie baby, one of my regulars has the hots for you. She saw you when you dropped Ma off at the shop last week. Want me to arrange a date?

E: What's she like?

L: A terrific person, very bright, sincere, nice sense of humor.

E: Forget it.

L: No, really, she's kind of cute, no tits but lots of hair.

E: Sounds like cousin Nathan.

[*Lilyan raises her middle finger to Eddie across the table*]

M: I'll think about going.

E: [*Prodding the sweet rolls Maryann bought*] It's like Saturday morning at Chock Full O' Nuts. Where are the bialies, the bagels?

F: Shhh. They're delicious.

[*Lilyan clutches her kimono and sashays over to the refrigerator in search of something else to eat. She doesn't know what she wants. Something. In a shaving mirror over the kitchen sink she sees a pimple on the side of her nose. She examines it carefully; it isn't ready to squeeze. It feels sore. Maybe it isn't a pimple.*]

F: What are you looking at?

L: It's a cancer, Ma.

F: Don't listen to her, God.

L: You think Lou could love a woman without a nose?

F: Bite your tongue, I want to see you bite your tongue.

L: I'm only kidding.

F: Bite.

L: [*Sticks out her tongue at Fay and bites it*] Satisfied?

Lilyan continues to the refrigerator. "Fat, fat, fat. That's me. I'm gonna write a book before you do, brother. *All My Faults.*" She waltzes back to the table with a container of sour cream, mimicking Fanny Brice singing "My Man." " 'With all your faults I love you still, I always will . . . Though your arms are full of hair, I still don't care. . . .' " She spoons a wobbly mass of sour cream on her plate. "Fat and old," she says, "twenty-one plus isn't good enough anymore. Now it's eighteen plus, maybe fourteen plus." She puts a dab of cream on Maryann's plate, and on her third trip to the refrigerator she leans out the window and shouts, "All you dirty old men out there, what's the desirable age this morning?"

Maryann: [*Mumbling incoherently*] Please, please, I'll get my bag.

Fay says, read me my horoscope for this month Lillie darling.

Lilyan opens the new issue of *Vogue.* She always reads her horoscopes in newspapers, magazines, penny machines. She likes a little bit of a head start, she says. She reads to Fay: "Your artistic nature may find a new expression on the seventh—hurry, before inspiration fades. On the ninth a surprise gives you direction when a new love suddenly appears. Try to initiate action over the seventeenth to twenty-third or at least use the eighteenth and nineteenth to augment official moves. Health: Beaming. Money: Prospects. Love: Positively."

Fay is surprised.

Lilyan's horoscope says that her love life will greatly improve on the eighth, fourteenth and twenty-sixth. (She will wait impatiently for those days, but then forget until the day is over and, looking back on the previous twelve hours, find no improvement.) It also says there will be a new element in her relationship with her beloved. Years ago, Lilyan would have been convinced that meant pregnancy. Even now there are times when she imagines a girl who would dance with a world-famous ballet company and a boy who would be a scientist with a Ph.D. from Harvard.

Lilyan: [to Maryann, grimacing] So what, it's only life, right? Big deal. Who cares?

Maryann thought, Me, me, I care.

She said, "Please let me do the dishes before I go." She would do her share as at a mission.

"Go where?" Fay asked, genuinely curious.

Maryann hadn't considered an answer. It was humiliating to admit she was going back to Chagrin Falls. She said something about a locksmith and a hotel.

"Why should you stay alone when you can stay with friends?" Fay asked. Maryann seemed puzzled. "Us. You have other friends in New York? Eddie will take you in the cab for a few hours this afternoon and you'll see New York. You want to, Mimi sweetheart? Of course you do."

She managed to say, "But I don't—" before Eddie interrupted.

"Why do you ask her questions if you're going to answer them for her?" Eddie said, reading stock market listings although he didn't own any.

"If I thought she knew the answer I wouldn't ask her. I used to go in the cab before I got sick. Eddie said I was better protection than a dog. You'll take her, Eddie."

He nodded, uninterested. His rudeness infuriated Maryann and she thanked Fay again for her unforgettable hospitality and said she had to go. (She couldn't imagine a more ludicrous idea than driving around with Eddie Bern in his cab.)

Lilyan said, "No friend of mine goes to a hotel. Besides, Lou is coming over to practice for tomorrow night. You have to meet him. Did I tell you we're doing a tryout at a friend's place Sunday night? He may sign us up to dance a couple of nights a week. You have to come, right? So it's settled. Go with Eddie and then you'll pick us up at Roseland later. I'll teach you a few steps."

On the phone, Lilyan said, "Allo, Lou?" and winked at Maryann. "Bébé, c'est moi, Liliane." She told him to be at the apartment around two o'clock and said that Eddie and Maryann would meet them later at Roseland. "Maryann, my girl friend from Sharon Falls. It's near Cleveland. She's staying with us for a few days. You'll like her, but not too much," she added with a giggle before hanging up. "My big lover," she said.

"Lou is a putz." Eddie was reading automobile ads.

"You're just jealous because he's a successful business-man."

"You're crazy. You think Eddie Bern envies a manufac-turer of plastic pocketbooks?"

Fay was between them. "Lou is a nice boy."

"He's a forty-eight-year-old man."

"At least you recognize he's a man."

"More man than you, shmuck," Lilyan screamed at him. "At least he lives his life instead of dreaming it!" Besides, who said Lou wanted to marry her? Or she him? Sometimes he did; sometimes he was content to live as they did. Right now he was content and she wasn't sure how *she* felt.

"Stop it this minute, Lillie!"

Maryann rushed to escape, scurrying around the kitchen, trying to pile the dishes in the sink, pretending it wasn't happening. They terrified her, talking as though they hated one another. ("Keep your voice mellifluous, children, it's a sign of respect." But Maryann knew it was not to excite the neighbors. The Morrisons had never discussed anything emotionally; how they felt had nothing to do with life, tasks, duties.)

Fay stood over them, muttering, "She could do a lot worse." Like not having anybody and then what would happen to Lillie when Fay died? It was bad enough that Eddie was still single, a beautiful boy like Eddie. She had never liked Sid to begin with but she got used to him; Lilyan should never have divorced him. Now Fay would have to leave the two of them alone; no one for them to love, to know when they came home, to know *if* they came home. A mother's normal anxieties were for Fay a matter of instant pain, anguish, terror. It made her heart beat faster and the strength leave her legs. She sat down.

"Now look what you did!"

"Her pills, in her pocket!"

Maryann shoved Eddie and Lilyan aside. She forced the pill under her tongue. Then she lifted Fay's legs on to another chair and loosened her clothes, all the while speaking softly: "You're fine dear, you'll be fine." She chaffed her hands lightly and stroked Fay's brow.

After a few minutes Fay said, "Of course I'm fine. Why shouldn't I be? You're a regular Anna Neagle, she played Florence Nightingale in a wonderful picture. Look how you knew what to do. You saved my life. You were sent from heaven. Mimella darling, see who wants more coffee and then you girls will go to the laundromat for me."

More coffee? The laundromat? Maryann was certain they were insane.

From behind the television page, Eddie held out his cup for Maryann to fill. She filled it. She also added a small amount of milk and one lump of sugar. Maryann noticed things like that. Eddie put the cup down abruptly; who the hell was she to know how many lumps he took?

"Where are you going?" Fay called after him that he wasn't finished yet. Did he have enough?

From somewhere down the hall he told her yeah yeah he had enough.

11

When Lilyan and Maryann returned from the laundromat Lou was in the living room watching television, an old sports film of Glenn Cunningham running the one-mile race in 1933. Lou was sitting on the edge of a chair, his body straining forward, impassioned, he alone propelling Cunningham's piston legs. "Go, go, you crazy son of a bitch!" he cried, even though it had all happened years ago and both Lou and Cunningham already knew the outcome.

Lilyan threw herself on him, wrapping him in her warm largeness just as Cunningham reached the finish line, and Lou missed the triumphant flutter of ribbon and the champion's final gasping strides.

Lilyan was in a good mood. After Eddie left for work, she and Maryann went to the laundromat where she put Maryann's rain-soaked clothes into the tumbler along with the Berns' wash.

It was nice to have Maryann along for company. They pushed aside some magazines (Lilyan glanced at *True Confessions* and *Modern Screen* and said, "I read them") and sat on the low shelf in the front store window.

"You'd think Eddie would do it sometimes but Fay won't let him. You know what she says? He's a man and has to work for a living. That's her answer. Women's lib passed my mother by. She's still in the days when men are men and women wash clothes. The whole macho shtick is crap. I bring in as much to the house as Eddie, sometimes more."

Cozily she told Maryann about the shop and Nick; about opening her own place someday; about dancing; about Lou; about dancing with Lou; about her life with Sid. She even admitted that she had grown sick of Sid and of her inability to become interested in law. "The truth of the matter is I never really understood any of it," she confided. Funny, she had never admitted this even to her best friend, Sylvie. It was as though she had waited for Maryann these past years so she could tell her, it came out that easily.

Resting in the Second Avenue laundromat, Maryann told Lilyan about the boys and Jack, her work at the hospital, the drive at the school for music equipment, the bridge games, tennis at the club, the endless trek back and forth to dentists and doctors and Little League games and flute lessons. She didn't mention Jack's trips and her concern, although she suspected Lil would have loved to have given her advice. Nor did she say that she listened to her own telling of her days as though it was an unfamiliar story. But it was a decent life; loving, safe, contained, busy.

"Mrs. Redbook." Lilyan said it with affection (and some envy? Lil wondered).

"What does *that* mean?" Maryann asked Lilyan, suddenly feeling hostile, although she knew and didn't like the knowing. She was the lady whose life depended upon her buying White Cloud tissue; who had Dash at the top of her list; who used Spic 'n' Span and was thrilled that even her husband noticed; whose spoon stood up in Hunts tomato sauce. One of the hundreds of thousands of women dedicated to getting the odors out of her kitchen.

Would she prefer Lil's unattached free-spirited life? Maybe. The thought was unexpected. Despite Fay's needs, Eddie's presence, Lilyan would never be dependent on a telephone call in the middle of the night from another city from a man with a ring around his collar. ("Sorry to call so late, honey, but it was a long meeting.") Nor would Lilyan wait for the reassurance of "Hey, I'm home!" like some windup doll come to life now that *they* were home.

And what would she do on Falls Road when the boys were grown and gone, Jack on a business trip, no one calling "I'm home!"?

She could see, there on Second Avenue, that small-town

streets were virtually empty of people. Out of her kitchen window Maryann saw cars. By their cars ye shall know them. A blue Dodge and there goes Mrs. Harris to the market again; the dark maroon Mercedes with Joe Babcock on his way to do some serious drinking at a safe distance; a dented Karmann Ghia and what's Teddy Wertmuller doing home from Kenyon? A white Chevy Caprice, hello and goodbye Mrs. Mansfield and is Mr. Mansfield out of town again?

Not too long ago Tommy packed his Cub Scout knapsack and said he was going to sleep out under the maple tree at the edge of the lawn because it was time he practiced "cutting the apron strings." She and Jack laughed until some tears fell from her eyes.

"Oh, honey, you've got a long way to go before the boys won't need you," Jack said.

That's not quite the point, Jack, she didn't say.

"Hey, Mrs. Redbook, let's see you smile."

Cha cha cha bop bop bop. The music on the radio reached Lilyan's hips before it reached her ears. "Yeh, yeh," she cried, cha cha cha bop bop bop. "Are you a good dancer?"

"What do you mean by good?"

"I'm good," Lilyan said confidently. "When we get home I'll teach you a few steps."

"Where's Ma?"

"Taking a nap."

"Maybe I better check," she said.

"She's alive! You'll wake her up trying to find out if she's asleep."

Lou didn't look the way Maryann had invented him. He was tall: she assumed he would be short. He had a fleshless narrow frame; she had imagined him round, even pudgy. His reddish-brown hair was a thick ripple of tight, wiry waves: Maryann had taken his baldness for granted. He was aware of Maryann's unconscious scrutiny and sheepishly rubbed a patch of eczema on his forehead.

"Other people get ulcers, heart attacks," he said. It was an apology. "I get a rash."

"Lou makes vinyl handbags, business isn't always too hot."

"I'm beginning to think it isn't business, maybe I'm allergic to the plastics."

"Don't let the words leave your mouth. You'll talk yourself out of a living."

"I hear you're from around Cleveland," he said to Maryann. "I used to sell to Bond's out there."

Maryann said she knew the store.

"Maybe you've seen my bags."

"I probably have, perhaps I even bought one," she said generously.

Lou said he didn't think so. He could tell in a minute that this woman was not one of his customers. But it was nice of her to say so.

Maryann liked Lou. She was sorry that Lilyan had told her he wanted to dance under the stars forever. It made him seem so vulnerable, not knowing that Lilyan revealed his soft yearnings to any stranger.

But of course Lou suspected that Lilyan did do that. He didn't mind. When he told her that he imagined them in each other's arms always, that he never felt so complete as when they were dancing together, it didn't matter that she laughed. He heard affectionate laughter. She didn't have to believe him. He knew it was true. Dancing with her made him feel whole. There were no fragments, no pieces. He had never felt that way before.

Lou believed in fate. He believed that it was his fate to manufacture cheap vinyl handbags after an uneventful four years at Queens College. That's where he met Irv Chawitz whose father was in handbags. Lou had changed his cost-accounting course from the morning to the afternoon class and met Irv, who became his best friend. If Lou had kept to his original morning schedule he would never have gotten so friendly with Irv and Irv's father wouldn't have given him a job during the summers. Lou often pondered on this and liked to trace his life back to what might have caused him to do one thing or another in the first place and then search even further back and mesh the past with a chain of ifs, of causes and effects, that led up to his life at whatever given moment.

The result was that Lou often stood immobilized on a street corner. Should he go uptown and across town by walking east on Twenty-eighth Street and then turn uptown on Fifth or should he walk north on Eighth and then east at Thirty-fourth?

It was Lou's theory that on this or that street he might (or might not) meet someone and some event that would change his life (luck). When he read accounts in newspapers or heard about innocent passersby being shot by an escaping holdup man or being knifed by a fourteen-year-old mugger, or being killed by a falling object loosened from its roof moorings, or being caught between the smashup of two cars, he invariably considered what would have happened if the victim walked a different route and so avoided the catastrophe. Or what if the victim had stopped to tie a shoelace, which changed the timing by mere seconds and in that way changed his entire life? Saved his life!

On the other hand, Lou was capable of positive thinking too. Fate was not always ill. Supposing he, Lou, turned the corner on Twenty-seventh Street instead of Twenty-eighth Street on his way to the office. Perhaps he would meet the buyer of bags from Woolworth's, a meeting that might lead to a big order; or his banker, who might decide, on the basis of the casual encounter, the pleasant small talk, to give him the loan, after all; or just after his wife left him, the blonde who had coffee at the luncheonette every morning at the same time he did and the spontaneous meeting lead to a dinner date and more.

He had not turned the corner at Twenty-seventh and never met the banker, the buyer, the blonde. But he did go to

Roseland one night instead of to his sister's house, where he played gin rummy with his brother-in-law every night since his wife had taken the children, one suitcase of clothes and a paper bag of toys and called him from her mother's apartment. (He didn't go to his sister's that evening because she called him at the office and said she really wanted to go to a movie with her husband, "Just the two of us tonight, for God's sake, Lou, enough!" Lou managed to conceal that fact in his amnesiac subconscious where he stored most of his wounds and chose to recall that particular evening as a fateful decision of his own.)

It was certainly a decision. He used to go to Roseland occasionally, guiltily; he loved to dance but he could never persuade his wife to accompany him. She considered it—dancing—nonintellectual and not worthy of the attention of a woman who had organized the literary club in their building.

That was the night that Lou saw Lilyan for the first time.

By now he was convinced that it was meant to be that his wife should leave him, that he should meet Lilyan, that he should love her.

"It's Eddie," Lilyan said.

Maryann's heart responded to the stacatto ring from the downstairs bell with a paradiddle of her own. She didn't want to go. It was an absurd notion and she would simply say no. In fact, as soon as Lou and Lilyan finished showing her their dance act she would leave.

Lilyan and Lou had cleared the center of the small living room and were dancing for Maryann. "Wait until you dance with Lou where there's more room," Lilyan said, doing a natural spin turn. "There's nothing like it, dancing. You could talk from today till Shrove Tuesday and you couldn't communicate like dancing. Show me a person who doesn't like to dance and I'll show you a tightass human being. What I can't dig are the kids dancing and never touching each other. It's like tripping on drugs, you're all alone. Where's the fun, right? But it's beginning to change and we knew it all the time, me and Lou."

"Did Lil tell you about the gig we have Sunday night?" Lou asked, while swiveling Lilyan into a triple spin. "At the Bass Fiddle on Second Avenue."

"The owner is an old friend of mine, Joe Beamish," Lilyan said, winking at Maryann over Lou's shoulder, "and he said we could try out there. We worked up an act, a quickstep medley with a mambo tempo in the middle. We'll knock 'em dead. The whole place will be dancing. That was always my aim in life, to bring back dancing two by two. You heard of Tony and Sally DeMarco? Veloz and Yolanda? Well now you've got Lilyan Bern and Lou Sheingold."

"I've heard of Bern and Sheingold, but not Veloz and Yolanda," Maryann laughed.

"Cute," Lilyan said. "Look at her, Lou, isn't she gorgeous when she laughs?" Spin and hesitation. "What will you wear Sunday night? I want you to look terrific. I'll make Joe give you the best table up front, you and Eddie."

Maryann and Eddie. "I'll be there with a friend," she said quickly. Who? She would call Joe Westcott, Aunt Ella; she would think of someone. She would go home where she belonged.

"Why do you need another guy when you've got Eddie?" Lilyan said.

She and Lou finished with their special finale: a slide to Charleston, to point, two Woodpeckers, four Crackerjacks, two more Woodpeckers, to point. After the four Crackerjacks, Lou insisted they do it again. He coaxed Lil's timing, "Papa*pah*, papa*pah*, papa*pah*." When the bell rang they had gone through the finale five times and still he wasn't satisfied.

Maryann said, "I can't go."

Lilyan's head was out the window. On the sidewalk, Eddie yelled, "Send her down! Make it fast!" Behind his double-parked cab, a man in a Lincoln Continental was jabbing the horn.

Upstairs, Maryann couldn't find her sunglasses and said she wouldn't leave without them; then she had to go to the toilet; then she said, "I don't really—"

"Just go, will you? We'll see you later at Roseland. Look at me." Lilyan twisted a few curls around Maryann's ears. Now they could hear two horns bleating.

"Take a sweater, you never know." That was Fay, a frail cry of misgiving from the bedroom, but Lilyan had pushed Maryann out the door.

12

Maryann stumbled into the seat next to Eddie, slamming the door on her dress. Eddie had already started the car and after yanking at the skirt surreptitiously she decided not to mention it.

"We'll head downtown," he said, "pick up a few fares, see where they take us. Then we'll have lunch at a special place I know." For no apparent reason that he knew of, Eddie's mood had changed. He felt not only better but expansive, even generous. "We'll get your luggage later and you can decide about a hotel then."

"You don't have to do this." Maryann, striving to sound aloof, was sullen.

"Don't be frightened, little girl," he mocked her.

"But aren't you supposed to be working?"

"Sure, but it's strictly up to me how much time I put in. I own the cab with another guy and we each keep what we make. I had a good day yesterday, so relax. Is everybody so uptight in Chagrin Falls?"

He turned the radio dial until he found a Schubert quintet and whistled with the violins, pausing occasionally for a soft, careless "Motherfucker," a friendly "Break a leg" tossed at other drivers and pedestrians.

"There's a building downtown near the Battery I want you to see. The entire side is a clock." Then he asked anxiously, "You're not the Grant's Tomb type, are you?"

Only last Saturday night he had met a chick from Syracuse at a party and the way they swayed on the swinging kitchen door like a pendulum, he called his friend Alan to line up his place for all of the next day. But what *she* wanted was to ride around town from the Statue of Liberty to the Cloisters, with a stop at Grant's Tomb, where she wept. It was really sweet, she sobbed, that Mrs. Grant was buried there too. Later, at Alan's place, it wasn't worth Grant's Tomb.

"No," Maryann said, "I've been there."

"That's good news," Eddie said seriously.

With and without passengers (one woman was indignant that someone sitting up front was getting what she called a free ride on her money and threatened to report him to the hack bureau, but Eddie explained that Maryann was his wife and he was "breaking her in, teaching her the ropes," he said, so that she could cover for him when he went into the hospital for this major operation and just in case he died, God forbid, their three kids wouldn't go hungry), they drove down Fifth Avenue, up Park, across to the West Side and back to the East.

For the most part Maryann saw façades of buildings—"That's 200 Fifth Avenue, only toy companies; the buyers fill the place around February when they buy for Christmas." At the Forty-second Street Library he double-parked precariously and sent her in to see the Berg Collection of first editions, rare books and documents. Eddie did a lot of his undergraduate work there and once worked out a caper to steal the original manuscript of T. S. Eliot's *The Waste Land*. In the garment center they were stalled behind behemoth trucks unloading separates and pants suits and escaped to the Avenue of the Americas, where he cruised along the street while Maryann ran in and out of wholesale flower and plant shops. She bought Fay a wandering Jew.

When Maryann's stomach began to grumble audibly, Eddie turned on his off-duty sign and headed downtown. They stopped for a brief glimpse of the New York University buildings, his alma mater (he sang "The Palisades"—"O grim gray Palisades;/Thy shadow upon the rippling Hudson falls" —with a Japanese accent) and then rested for a few minutes in Washington Square Park, sitting on a bench, where Eddie fed peanuts to the squirrels and Maryann and talked about Henry James.

"Why did you stop writing?" Maryann asked curiously.

"I didn't stop. I *am* a writer." Who did she think she was, telling him what he was and what he wasn't? That ticked him off. "The cab is for bread. A convenience."

"Last night you said you were a cab driver."

"Last night, last night, I'm disappointed in you. What better disguise for a writer than the role of a cab driver? I move around the city dealing with remarkable events, complex plots, rich characters. My book is practically writing itself." He waited; there was a certain type of person who asked what the book was about.

Maryann asked what the book was about. Eddie sighed. "I consider that a very naïve question, but if you insist, I will describe it in one sentence. It's about a guy and two of his friends and what happens to them in the spring of their lives."

"And?"

"And what? And is a conjunction signifying more to follow. There's no and. I'm not one of your performing writers who gives a recitation of the plot and reads whole chapters to anyone who will listen. It's a known fact that you diffuse the emotional impact that way. Once having said it, why write it? But my whole plot is out there," he said, waving vaguely at the dogs, the derelicts, the chess players, the clusters of dying people and the newly born.

"Here," she corrected him.

"Here for you, there for me. I am an observer of life. In fact, you are with a very exceptional fellow."

Three small boys rooted themselves in front of the park bench and stared at Maryann and Eddie. Eddie said, "Beat it," and the smallest boy replied, "Fuck you," and they ran away screaming in an ecstasy of fearlessness.

"Do you have a lot of kids?"

"Two."

"That's a lot."

"My husband felt—"

"Not interested in your husband," he interrupted. It's not

that he wanted to ball her, but women's husbands didn't concern him.

A low blow, Maryann decided; she should have gone home. "I'm not surprised that *you* never married," she said with some meanness and a sudden irrational annoyance with Jack for putting her in this predicament.

"I suffer from acedia," Eddie said, looking at her gravely, delighted with the angry splotches on her cheeks. "That means sloth and indifference, it's a very selective condition." Most married women talked about marriage to him; he considered it a kind of flirtation and he could feel a few moist locks of hair framing his forehead. "Do you know how many times I could have married the wrong girl? And where would I be now? Paying alimony, trying to figure out what to do with my kids on Sunday, picking them up in some lobby because I didn't want to deal with my ex-wife upstairs. I've seen too much of it with my friends. Listen," he grinned, "I figure I have until forty. Then the marriage will be arranged with an old family with good connections and a substantial dowry. My young bride, a ripe virgin, will come to our bridal chamber with eyes downcast, glancing at me shyly through thick lashes, hiding her innocent and primordial lust." Maryann could feel his warm peanutty breath as he leaned toward her. "How does that sound?" he asked.

"Perfect," she murmured, disconcerted by the few moist locks of hair framing his forehead. "Why wait until you're forty?"

When Eddie's friends kidded him about living at home, he said it gave Fay something to do. It was true. She ironed his shirts and prepared lamb chops twice a week and told him what a terrific catch he was for some beautiful and intelligent and rich girl, but when? when? and would she live to see a grandchild? That's what she said on her bad days when she felt ill and threatened. On her good days she assured him he was still young and there was plenty of time.

Of course there was Judy. Once he thought that Judy was the only one and when she died that was the end of love for

Eddie Bern. He had enshrined her in a short story (that's all
for Judy?) and the fact that it was the only story he ever
published in a good literary magazine had some meaning for
him.

His last gift to her? Her last gift to him?

At the time it was also an eloquent embodiment of his one
man-one woman theory. But in the last three or four years
he had begun to look around again. He convinced himself
that maybe Judy, may she rest in peace, was not the only
one, after all. He was now willing to accept the fact that
there was no singular and exclusive personification of the
inchoative love he felt inside, as though it were an entity
waiting to be unwrapped and lavished on . . . whom? Each
time someone gave him a new number, his heart soared
with the hope of the ineluctable meeting. Was this the one?

He divided his girls into three categories. First Category:
the girls he didn't want to see again after the initial date.
Second Category: the girls he didn't run to meet but, on the
other hand, he didn't want to be late. Third Category: the
one he couldn't wait until he saw again, springing that last
block, those last few steps, and then flying, jumping, leaping
into her arms and she into his.

It was interesting to him that the girls in the Second
Category lasted longer in terms of time and relationship than
those in the Third Category. Though he leaped toward the
Third Category girls at first, he would then do something,
not do something, say something, not say something, goad
them into not doing, not saying, saying, doing.

Whatever it was, he didn't want to know.

Anyway, he now had this new theory. "What do you think?
Is there only one person in the world you could love and
marry or are there many?"

Maryann thought of her universe in Ohio and surely there
was only Jack. But a sudden perversity made her wonder
what would happen (for instance, would the sky fall down,
Chicken Little?) if she said, There may be many. She was a
contestant searching for the right answer. Would she get the

Rolls-Royce Corniche or the year's supply of Pretzel Stix? She had a brief, gripping moment of anxiety and decided not to take big chances.

"I certainly believe in the destiny of one person," she said. "Now you're equivocating." (She got the Pretzel Stix.) "Of course, *this* is destiny. You are, you're here, Descartes and all that shit. But D. H. Lawrence once said that there isn't just one woman a man can marry. That all over the world there are human beings we could live with happily, raise children with, make a life with. I'll bet at this minute there are five girls in Rome I could be happy with, maybe two in Canton, a dame in Bombay. Take yourself. I'll bet there's a guy in Frankfurt you could have married and lived with and been happy as a shnitzel. Maybe three in Athens, two in Venice, even one in Vestspitsbergen."

But if there was someone else for her in Vestspitsbergen then there was someone else for Jack in Vladivostok, in Bahía, in Montreal. The thought was unbearable. "No," she said firmly, "if you're talking about destiny, about fate, the fact still remains that we *do* marry So-and-So in whatever city and therefore *that* person becomes one's destiny."

She was very intense about it. Eddie was interested. Suddenly she was more than good-looking: she was beautiful. Well, beautiful was going too far. A little adorable perhaps. Eddie considered the possibility that she was the one who would shape his shapeless life. It didn't matter that she had a husband in Ohio. Nothing was permanent, nothing was forever. She was probably into one of those trial separations where she had to get away to think things through.

So how about one in Chagrin Falls? The shiksa from Chagrin Falls. He liked the alliteration; it sounded like something from a Yiddish repertory company on Second Avenue.

Now there was an undeniable rumble from Maryann's stomach. Eddie was very apologetic and promised a direct ride to lunch, no fares.

But en route, he said it would be a mitzvah—a good deed,

he explained—to pick up the small man with a large package (Maryann, up front, was trying to stifle the gurgles) and take him to a dowdy brick building on Mott Street. Eddie told Maryann that subcontractors rented the lofts inside and he insisted she run up a few flights just to take a look. She clattered through dismal hallways, peering into rooms serried with sewing machines stitching low-priced ladies' ready-to-wear; it was a coffee break and the metal stairways echoed with laughing, clicking Spanish tongues.

" 'Just tell me what street compares with Mott Street in July'—" Eddie warbled when she returned. No one could say he wasn't the romantic type.

Maryann, who had bent, shaped, molded herself around Jack, John and Tommy like some tripodic freak, suddenly sat up straight and laughed. She was on Mott Street in July.

"Now you got it," Eddie grinned. "Relax. Make believe you live in Lapland and the long dark winter is over."

How about one in Lapland?

13

The special place for lunch that Eddie promised was the Essex Street Market. Four square blocks, a thick forest of stalls covered with food and redolent with odors.

Eddie ignored Maryann's small retching sounds and urged her to take it all in—the chickens, ducks, sides of beef and lamb, whole pigs and rabbits, all snared on massive hooks. Resting quiescently on pillows of ice, mouths ovaled in a last futile gasp for air, were carp, striped bass, mullets, whitings, butterfish. Maryann breathed in the monstrous stink of food and was bedazzled by a display of salted pig's ears, pigtails, pig's feet, octopus, squid, turtle meat. (Who were these people who ate this food? Where did they live? Why hadn't she met them before? Known them? Where did they come from? Whom did they love?)

Bins of hard candies and nuts; pyramids of apples, plums, apricots, cherries, tangelos; loaves of white bread, hard-crusted, soft and doughy; black breads, wheat breads, rye breads, rolls, cakes, buns, cookies. Stockings. Books. A mass display of the Virgin of Guadalupe and figures of Christ in many sizes baring a bleeding heart. A radio repair service.

Eddie bought them lunch at a high, steaming counter: two gaucho pies and one pastelillo each, served and eaten off a greasy slip of slithery waxed paper. Although she was weak with hunger, Maryann could barely nibble at the outer crust and Eddie was exasperated.

"For Chrissakes, woman, you're not at Stouffer's. Here is a hundred years of kikes and wops and spicks and coons. React, goddammit! Finally you're in America!"

At a counter displaying dream books and prayer beads, he

bought her a vial of love potion as a souvenir. "You never know," he said.

For dessert they ate glâcé peaches and candied pineapples with sticky fingers reaching into one paper bag while walking outside among the sidewalk clothes racks on Orchard Street. Driven by a cacophony of Spanish music, Maryann bought a yard of fabric, flagrantly woven with metallic silver among threads of turquoise, orange and robin's-egg blue. She felt extravagantly dream-borne, as irrepressible as the colors and the music. She thought it the most exotic fabric she'd ever seen. (Years later she found it at the bottom of her lingerie drawer and couldn't recall the precise emotions of that moment when she bought the piece of cloth.)

Before they returned to the taxi, Eddie bought ice cream cones to finish the meal. They sat in the cab quietly; Eddie, with side glances, was entranced by Maryann's flickering tongue caressing and reshaping the ball of ice cream. She gives great cone, he mused.

Eddie put the cab in the parking lot on West Fifty-second Street next to the Roseland Ballroom. He seemed to have forgotten all about Maryann's luggage or checking her into a hotel and Maryann forgot to remind him.

14

In the lobby, Maryann stood in front of a display of shoes momentously balanced on shelves; the gravity of the exhibition emphasized by the locks on the glass doors. Dan Dailey's moccasins, Pat Rooney's pointed toes, Mae Murray's white satin pumps, Betty Grable's spike heel sequin mules; the dancing shoes of Tony DeMarco, Ray Bolger, Adele Astaire, George Raft. It was a final resting place.

Eddie led her into the main ballroom where a band was playing a bouncy version of "You're the Cream in My Coffee." There was a seductively soft swoosh of feet on the hardwood floor.

"Lilyan calls it the sound of people feeling lovely," Eddie said wryly, with a rare glimmer of affection.

Garlands of red and purple velvet hung in swags, framing the bandstand. Above was a heaven of overhead spotlights and on the walls, murals of violins, French horns, saxophones, clarinets, harps, all etched in gold.

Lou and Lilyan were dancing; Lil waved happily and Lou saluted them with an extravagant dip. On the dance floor Lou was a commanding figure, twirling Lilyan with only the slightest pressure, taking half steps, a hesitation, a sudden slide twice instead of once. Lou's feet moved impeccably, telling his body he was a man who counted for something. Lilyan followed faultlessly (big beefy Lilyan), fitting her inclinations to his, willing, faithful, trusting. In concentration, her lips were pursed to the size of a dainty fragile doll's mouth.

Eddie shrugged. "It's a skating rink, their game, their sport."

The couples on the floor astonished Maryann. Eddie told her that many of them rarely saw each other outside of Roseland, yet, she saw, they seemed to dance together with the sureness and skill of each knowing the other body's most intimate impulses.

A woman, six feet tall, sailed in front of Maryann's eyes like a mast; in her hand she clutched a small evening bag. Her partner's head rested against her sternum, his face serene, as he led the graceful vessel through the sea of couples. Near the rail, as though it were a sanctuary from the force of humanity, an older man, bulky and shapeless, his pants cuffs flapping carelessly around faded socks, his dentures revealed in a beatific smile that was almost a grimace, moved his head from side to side in small rhythmic motions, like a battery-run toy. His partner pivoted from the palm of his right hand held aloft. Her stomach, round and aged, showed comfortably from a long knit dress with a cloth gardenia pinned to it and her right arm was outstretched in an achingly chaste gesture. They danced with flawless cadence. Around them swirled young couples with beards, mustaches, ponytails, slim, stylishly dressed, and in some kind of rapture. Many seemed to be professional dancers, gliding in long strides, moving in a mime of intense grace. It was a mélange of lilting bodies and Maryann thought, No one told me it would be this way.

Lilyan, beaming, hugged Maryann and organized a table where they ordered coffee, cheesecake and danish pastries "just in case" Lilyan said. Maryann sipped a dry sherry and marveled that Eddie could ingest any more food.

A soft-fleshed woman hurried by but stopped long enough to give Lilyan a peck on her cheek and Eddie a lingering leer. "Better not stand up or I'll grab you you-know-where!" she chortled. Maryann was amused to see Eddie's face flush.

Lilyan said, "How are the kids?"

"Both in show biz, you know, they love it. They're doing a lot of jingles."

Lilyan sighed and asked, "Does she take ballet?"

"No, sings a little, dances a little, a chip off the old block," the woman said, doing a buck-and-wing finale toward the door.

"I used to double-date with her when we were in high school. She looks awful," Lilyan said to Maryann, and then caught a glimpse of herself in a mirrored wall. "I don't look so good either."

Maryann's first dance was with a stranger, a man with a thin mustache who came over to their table and asked her if she would like to dance.

"No," she cried with a sudden rush of terror. "I don't dance, I watch."

"Didn't you see me dance?" he asked, his fingers spread at his midriff, his body suddenly undulating as though he had pressed a vital switch.

Everyone urged her to dance; the man seemed baffled that she had rejected his offer. It was a gentle fox-trot and he sang in her ear, "A pretty girl is like a syn-phony!" She was certain he could feel her body tremble, leaning bravely against his unknown contours. Later she was astonished that he had carried her along effortlessly and that her legs seemed to follow him with an unaccustomed ease. (Who was he, this stranger, to make dancing seem so easy?)

He brought her back to Eddie; Eddie accepted his thanks. "Anytime," he said to the man.

Whoever came over to the table was invited by Lilyan and Lou to be at Joe Beamish's Bass Fiddle the following night around ten o'clock. They needed the support of friends to clap it up, she said.

"If they like us, I figure we can do two shows Sunday nights and Wednesday nights," she said. "If we build up a following we'll do Saturday too. Right Lou?"

"Quit it, Lil, they might not like us. Don't expect too much."

"Why not? People have been dancing alone for the last ten, fifteen years. They need someone like us to give them a shove, show them how to get close. Lou, baby, they've been waiting for us. Dancing is the big thing today and we were here first. We'll show them how."

Eddie danced with Maryann finally. He wanted it to be the right song, he said, ignoring mambos, tangos, waltzes, hustles. When the band played "Love Walked Right In" he stood up, whirled around on an imaginary cane and elaborately escorted her to the dance floor. There he clowned a bit at first and did more of his Fred Astaire imitation (the tilted top hat, the cuffs, a little soft-shoe) until Lil called from the table, "Dance already!"

His step was a shuffling box step. Maryann stepped on his foot a few times and they lost the beat twice. Finally he put both arms around her and they swayed on one spot. Maryann's body tensed and she pulled away imperceptibly from her waist down, but Eddie pressed closer.

When they got back to the table, one of his old girl friends had joined them. Lil had fixed him up with many of the Roseland regulars.

"How's it going?" he asked, although he wasn't really interested.

"Now I'm trying hypnotism," she said to him. "What do you think?"

"Could work."

Lilyan leaned over and said, "Maryann this is Barbara; Barb this is Maryann, a close family friend from Ohio. Barbara can't dance," Lilyan confided to Maryann.

"I don't know why you aggravate yourself," Lou said to Barbara, "do the best you can and enjoy it."

"He's right, you're overreacting," Eddie said.

"I'm a perfectionist, you should know that Eddie." That surprised Eddie.

"She went to psychiatrists two different times in her life." Lilyan told Maryann. "Nothing helped."

"I'm a professional klutz," Barbara explained to Maryann. "But this time I think I'm into something. The hypnotist says he'll have me dancing in three sessions. I said I just want to dance like Lilyan Bern, so he said who's Lilyan Bern, so I said come to Roseland with me after I'm hypnotized and see, so he said it's a deal. So he's coming."

Lou had leaned over to ask Maryann, "Do you know—?" and Maryann nodded, she knew what a klutz was. Often she felt like one. Lou called to Barbara as she left, "Let us know when the hypnotist is coming and we'll be here."

Lilyan sighed. "Inside she's graceful, inside she's full of rhythm, that girl. Outside it's the two-step and she can't hear the beat. Believe me, she'll never dance."

Another girl came to the table and stood in front of Eddie. "I'm going to Santa Fe to start a band. Goodbye," she said to him sternly. (Once she had been a girl in the Third Category.)

When she left, Eddie murmured: "What do you think she meant by goodbye?"

It took all her courage for Maryann to ask Lou if he would dance with her. But Lou was already offering her his arm after Lilyan pinched his thigh under the table and motioned toward Maryann.

Lilyan was right: Maryann floated in Lou's arms. He was kind and masterful and made her feel that she wasn't a klutz.

They swayed in front of the bandstand; it was a familiar sensation of school proms and country-club dances. "I can see it would be easy to pretend that you're in a time capsule and nothing has changed," she said, wondering how it happened that she was being held by a man named Lou Sheingold and dancing in New York.

"You think that's why people come here? I'm not so sure you're right."

"Why do *you* come here?"

"No big explanation. I come to feel close to someone and to dance. Two things I like the most."

On the way out, Lilyan said to Maryann, "Did you see this?" They stopped in front of a large wall plaque with hundreds of names listed. "See? 'Roseland Dance City in Honor of the Married Couples Who First Met Here.' Of course, people don't come here to meet anyone, you know what I mean, but if it happens they wouldn't say no." She tucked her arm through Maryann's as they walked out. "Lou and I will be on that list if we get married. I don't know." She brooded. "Did I tell you I'm thinking of opening my own shop? I guess in the end I'm happy this way," she whispered to Maryann. "We dance, we see each other, we shtup"—the word startled Maryann—"I still have my own life. Shit, who knows what to do?" She was in a maybe-yes period; Lou, she thought, might be in a what's-the-rush period. Or was it the other way around?

They went to Ginny's building to get Maryann's luggage. Lilyan said she wouldn't hear a word about Maryann staying at a hotel, not a word, or even trying to get into Ginny's penthouse apartment. "The hell with it. What do you need it for," she wanted to know, "when you have us?"

They stopped at a delicatessen at Second Avenue and Seventy-seventh Street for sandwiches. Lou and Eddie ate all the pickles and sour tomatoes on the table before the waiter took their order. Maryann asked what was the difference between corned beef and pastrami.

The waiter said, "I'll tell you a secret about corned beef and pastrami. Beef is beef. But it's like ordering a suit. Some people like gray pinstripes, another guy likes brown with tan, another guy wants a blue herringbone, but it's still a suit, right? So what'll you have?"

Maryann and Lilyan said they would have the corned beef on rye; Lou wanted the no. 7 with nova, sturgeon, lettuce, tomatoes and Bermuda onion and Eddie said he'd have a blue pinstripe and hold the lapels.

SUNDAY

15

Lilyan was snoring softly when Maryann awakened at nine, still feeling guilty about the night before. Lou was about to leave them when it occurred to Maryann that perhaps Lilyan might want to go home with him, or maybe it was customary for him to stay at the Bern apartment on Saturday night.

"Don't let me stop you from—I mean, if you want to—" She was furious with Eddie who mimicked her, asking, "Stop her from what? What does she want to?" Finally it was Lou who told Eddie to knock it off.

"It's okay, baby," Lilyan said to Maryann, "Lou has to catch an early bus to New Jersey. It's his visiting day with his kids so it's fine, believe me."

Then Eddie surprised them by suggesting that he would drive everybody down to Freehold later in the afternoon and pick up Lou; that way they would be sure he would get to Joe Beamish's place on time. "And you want to show Maryann some of the spots outside New York, don't you?"

Lilyan winked at Lou and later, before they fell asleep, Lilyan said to Maryann, "You must be doing something right, kid. It's the first time Eddie ever offered to pick up Lou down in Jersey." Maryann closed her eyes in a moment of panic: it was not her purpose to do anything right.

Fay was in the kitchen reading the Sunday papers. "My early bird," she smiled at Maryann. "Sit down, I have coffee all ready. I made breakfast for Eddie before he left for work.

He's so ambitious lately. When you know him better, you'll see he's some guy."

"He's going to take us driving this afternoon and we'll pick up Lou in New Jersey."

"You see? Eddie's very generous, everyone always says that about Eddie and so easy to get along with."

While Maryann had coffee and toasted bagels with cream cheese, Fay regaled her with stories about people whose names she didn't remember and who Maryann didn't know in any case.

"My very closest friend, wait, her name will come to me in a minute, had a cancer operation God forbid it should happen to anybody. She was left with no intestines to speak of, and the doctors said she would die in six months we shouldn't know such things but look at that, she's still with us, among the living," Fay said gaily. "And this happened two years ago. No, maybe it's a year. Wait, I myself was in the hospital at that time, and that was a year and a half. A year and a couple of months. Whatever. Are you afraid to die?" she asked Maryann, bringing another toasted bagel to the table.

Maryann was now accustomed to anything Fay might say and considered the question seriously. "I think about it. But I'm not afraid of my death so much as afraid of leaving my sons and my husband. I guess he'd marry again"—that was hard to say—"and I worry about whether she would be good to my children."

Aha! Fay thought. I was right, if it was a true and eternal love her husband wouldn't get married again. He would worship at the shrine of her memory. To Maryann she said darkly, "Don't worry about husbands, they have a way of managing. But the sons. I knew you were my kind of person, worrying about your children. A real mother. I worry about my own kids. Believe me, age doesn't mean anything, a mother never stops worrying. I wish Lilyan would marry Lou already. And Eddie"—she glanced at Maryann—"such a talented boy. He's only in his thirties but he should get married. How old are you? Between us, I wouldn't tell."

"Just about forty," said Maryann.

"I would never know it, you look like a girl. If you ask me as a woman, not as a mother, my Eddie should marry a woman a year or two older than he."

"Why, for heaven's sake?"

"You don't know him the way I do. A mature woman would know how to care for him," and then she hurried to add, "of course he would care for her too, it goes without saying."

"It's only my opinion, Fay," Maryann said gently, "but Eddie strikes me as the kind of person who might always be not quite ready for marriage."

"Then how will I die if there is no one to take care of him?" Fay demanded.

"Don't die," Maryann said, patting her hand.

"That's easy for you to say. Well, who knows, maybe Eddie was smart not to get married all these years. I try not to dwell on the bad parts, but my own marriage, a passionate love affair believe me, was not always happy. After we got back from our honeymoon in—I'll tell you in a minute" —she thought awhile—"to tell you the truth I don't remember where we went on our honeymoon—he started immediately with a temper. He never showed me such a temper before the wedding. So I showed him a temper. You don't play around with Fay. From then on it was mostly cats and dogs but we never parted. To the end we loved each other. I think."

Maryann said, "I'm sure he loved you very much."

Fay shrugged; it hardly mattered anymore. "And *your* husband?" she asked.

"Of course," Maryann said. Why couldn't she say yes, yes, Jack loves me very much? How much reassurance did she need?

Of course. Fay wondered what of course meant.

Fay cried suddenly, "Remember when you first came to us I said I had a story to tell. It's a real love story. You want to hear it? You're sure? So okay."

Fay enjoyed telling this story. She moved the cream cheese and container of milk to make room for her elbows.

16

Did you ever know of Lilyan Tashman? she asked Maryann.
No. Lilyan Tashman was simply a gorgeous and beautiful
blond actress with big blue eyes. She was a Ziegfeld Follies
beauty in the days of Marion Davies—remember I said
Marion Davies to you a long time ago? It's fate that you
and my Lilyan should meet. Of Marilyn Miller, of Ina Claire.
All people you never heard of. Lilyan was a girl from a very
fine Jewish family, very devoted, in Brooklyn, very smart,
she was going to Hunter College to be a teacher. So one day
Ziegfeld found her in a restaurant, and lo and behold she
becomes a Follies beauty. Okay so far?
   (With cupped hands she put Lilyan Tashman aside.)
   Now meanwhile, Edmund Lowe was a struggling actor on
the stage, trying for the big break, and somehow, I'm not
clear on this, Lilyan Tashman helped him. She was the type
of person who was a regular trouper and a really swell pal.
Well, then Edmund Lowe went to Hollywood to go into
the movies and he was a big success. He was famous for
wearing a top hat and a very long silk scarf and he was
so handsome you could die looking at him. So time passes,
to make a long story short, and Lilyan Tashman wants to
go into the movies too.
   (Fay reached for Lilyan Tashman and placed her next to
Edmund Lowe.)
   She goes to Hollywood and says to Edmund Lowe, I was
your friend and now you be my friend. And not only was he
a friend to her but they fell madly in love and they got
married. Hollywood in those days was a Gehenna, you know
what that means? A dirty place. But not Tashman and Lowe.
They had a perfect marriage, they were the ideal couple.

People called their marriage an epic of love. Only once was there a breath of scandal that breathed on them. The papers said that Lilyan found some woman in her husband's dressing room and she beat her up, did you ever hear anything so ridiculous about a girl who went to Hunter College to be a teacher? Later they said it was the other woman who beat up Lilyan. Anyway, it was an ugly business and I didn't believe a word of it. It was a shame that it should even have been mentioned in the papers. It was pure jealousy, people were jealous that they were so happy. Anyway, Lilyan had lots of parts but she was always the second leading lady even though, believe me, she had more talent in her little finger than I don't know who had in I wouldn't even mention where. Lowe was a very fine player too; I remember him in *What Price Glory*, what a picture, and he played his part so good. Well, the years passed, seven, eight, and their lives were like a fairy tale. Until one day, and this is what I'm leading up to, she got sick. They said she dieted too much, but that wasn't true. She had a tumor. She had been sick for a year but kept working anyway, a regular trouper like they said. I remember, she was making a picture at the old Biograph Studios in the Bronx and once I went up there to see if I could sneak in just to look at her but they wouldn't let me in and I waited awhile outside but she didn't come out. Oh! and she dressed like a vision of loveliness, that was another thing. She had the most beautiful clothes and she was always on the top of the Best Dressed List. Gloria Swanson and Constance Bennett—you know them?—always tried to beat her but they never could be no. 1. No one could touch her when it came to clothes. Anyway, what can I tell you, she had a tumor, and like the very next day after her first starring picture opened—finally she was going to be the star in *Wine, Women and Song*—she died. I don't know why I remember these things, I can't even remember my sister-in-law's name, but these things I remember. *Wine, Women and Song*, that was the title. Do you get the significance? Such irony. They tried to operate but it didn't help. Lilyan Tashman died March 21, 1934. Ask me the exact day my husband died, I couldn't tell you. It was all over the front pages. The funeral was two days later at the Universal Funeral Chapel when they were on Fifty-second Street near Lexington. I went, naturally. She was buried in a blue dress, I didn't see it but they wrote it up in the papers the next day, and a rabbi from Temple Emanu-El conducted the services and Eddie Cantor—*you* know who *he* is—gave the eulogy. I didn't see him, I was outside, you couldn't get in, there were so many celebrities, over four hundred stars of stage, screen and radio. Sophie Tucker, Mary Pickford, Fanny Brice, Mae Murray, Mr. *and* Mrs. William Randolph Hearst, Jr.—you name it, everyone was there. On the loudspeaker Eddie Cantor said that in twenty years he knew her he never heard her say anything bad about anybody. That's the type of person she was. When I die I'll be a happy woman if someone says that about me. I never saw such a crowd, pushing and shoving and carrying on, you'd think the Queen of England died. And what I didn't tell you, I was saving it for last, I was pregnant with my Lillie but I didn't know it was my Lillie, naturally, and I was due in two weeks. I didn't tell my husband I was going to the funeral, he would have locked me up in the apartment, but I couldn't not go, right? This wonderful person. It was funny how I felt about her, like one of my own family, like she was my sister. A real-life tragedy. I still can't get over it.

(Fay tore off a piece of bagel and chewed pensively.)

Anyway, the place was crazy, jammed. The police had to hold everybody back. They stopped all the traffic, although in those days traffic wasn't what it is today. But even that part wasn't so bad, what happened was that I made a mistake and I went to the cemetery too. My friend had a car, I wouldn't go alone, and a whole bunch of us piled in and we went out to Brooklyn with the funeral. Thousands and thousands and thousands of people were there, it was something I'll never forget. They had to keep the people from rushing to the grave to pick the flowers off the casket. Yellow roses. Can you imagine? Mostly women, hysterical. Like animals. I never saw anything like it before and God should be good to me I should never see it again. Anyway, somebody gave me a push, a real zetz, it was lucky I didn't fall into the grave, but I fell over a bush, backward, thank God, not on my stomach. I was so big with my Lillie, two policemen had to lift me up, that's how big I was. I thought I would be trampled to death. My husband would have murdered me if I had been killed. Anyway, the following week my Lillie was born. What else could I name her, right? The poor woman had no children, would there ever be a name for her? So I did it, me, Fay, I gave her a name. In those days there were stars named Constance, Joan, Nancy, Ruth, Bebe, Madge, Greta, Janet, Elissa, Dolores. Also Ginger but I never liked those pictures, those Fred Astaire and Ginger Rogers pictures. I know everybody likes them but to me they were nonsense. It was always the same story; *he* thought *she* was somebody else and *she* thought *he* was somebody else and I always felt like standing up in the theater and saying so tell him who *you* are and *you* tell her who *you* are and that's that.

So Lillie was born. Then five years later my son was born. I tell everybody he's named for my father's grandfather Eliyu but he's really named for Edmund Lowe. Do you get the significance? I brought them together again, Lilyan Tashman and Edmund Lowe.

Fay shook her head absentmindedly. She hadn't told the story in such a long time.

"Well?" she roused herself. "Is that a love story or is that a love story?"

"What happened to Edmund Lowe?" Maryann asked.

"Oh, he cried a lot, his heart was broken of course, but he played on in pictures for many years. He was a trouper too." Then she whispered, "Sometimes I think I brought a curse on Eddie by naming him for a living person. Do you think so?"

"Why is that a curse?" Maryann asked, surprised. "People usually name a baby after the living."

"Not by us," Fay said. "I have a lot to teach you."

17

Fay sent Maryann to see if Lilyan was alive. She found her sprawled across the bed, the airless room in a haze of floating motes.

"It's almost noon, Lil, shouldn't you be getting up?"

"Yeah." She didn't move. "I have to do my nails, my hair. You want me to do yours?" she asked listlessly. She pulled herself up and groaned. "I got up before but it all looked so good"—waving at the malaise of musty bedclothes—"I went back to bed. How do you feel?"

"Fine. Why?"

"I don't feel too well."

"Maybe it's something you ate last night."

"We both had the corned beef."

"It could have been a particular piece."

"Yeah, I'll be okay. Don't mention it to Fay, she'll drive me bananas. She'll think it's a tumor."

In the kitchen, Lilyan poured a cup of coffee and asked, "What were you two rapping about? You never stopped."

"Love, marriage," Fay sighed.

"That old twosome," Lilyan said, weary.

"Since when are you against love and marriage?" Fay wanted to know.

"If I knew what it was I'd know if I was for it or against it. These days nobody tells you anything straight out. If you love somebody, do you get married or aren't you supposed to? They make you feel it's against the law. The kids today live together fucking and sucking like they had a marriage license." Fay murmured a protest; Lilyan ignored her. "And then look at me, your new independent woman, free to do anything I want. It's fantastic. I was married once and every day I thank God someone else is in Sid's bed. Okay, a new world, Goldie? So why when there was a call on the loud-speaker in Grand Central Station, 'Dr. Wright, Dr. Wright, come to the information booth,' fifty-seven girls came running, including me?"

Maryann waited.

Lilyan said with kindness, "It's a joke. What I'm trying to say is I think the whole world is crazy. Sex is hanging out like your pupik, women are liberated, nobody's a spinster, it's like they took the word out of the dictionary, but, still, some poor girl in California kills herself on the radio because she isn't married. And the society pages, have you seen them? They're still filled with engagements and wedding announcements. And not just little get-togethers. Big catered affairs, hot and cold hors d'oeuvres, squab, presents, pots and pans, silverware. The bride's patterns are still registered at Tiffany's. Would you believe it? And babies. I don't think the statistics have caught up yet. More and more people are having babies. It's starting up again. That maternity shop on Madison Avenue just expanded, they needed more space. You think they're investing for nothing?" With raging intensity she piled cream cheese and raspberry jam on a bagel. "Remember that your friend Lillie told you. Ten years from now there won't be enough classrooms because no one noticed all the big bellies on the street. No one knows what they really want and I'm beginning to think that we're being handed a pile of shit by the media."

"Lillie!"

"Shit. If you don't like it, don't listen."

"You don't feel well?"

"I feel fine, leave me alone!"

"Then I'm going to take a nap," Fay said coldly.

"Apologize to her." Maryann was scandalized.

"I apologize, Ma," Lilyan murmured to no one. She took another bagel. "So what do you think?" she asked Maryann.

"I think it's funny to hear you talk this way when I've been envying you your, well, lack of dependency—let's call it that—on anyone or anything."

"Don't be too sure about it. Remember I'm the great believer in dancing two by two."

"Yes, I know, but you don't seem to be"—what?—"needy," she said finally. As I am.

"Are you telling me you've got the sorries because you married and had kids?" Lilyan was both derisive and incredulous. "*My* Mrs. Redbook?"

"I didn't say that." Maryann was sharp. She remembered a woman at the airport Friday night, surrounded by four crying children and the woman scolded, "I don't have to listen to you nagging at me, I wasn't born with you kids, you know." It made Maryann laugh at the time but it was true enough. Maryann wasn't born with her boys either but her boys were born with *her*. And what should she have done? Given up raising them, being with them, in exchange for some odd job, so that she could get out of the house? Or bring them closer to the bigger house, the status move to Gates Mills? She wasn't a musician or a scientist or a legal brain. And Jack. Should they have not married at all, like latter-day prophets, anticipating in the nineteen fifties the life-style of the seventies? What else could they have done in those days: they loved each other. (Had she said that before?) They got married and had children and never knew that society would demand that she should be liberated and Jack be in male menopause at forty.

"What's the difference," Lilyan said, suddenly tired. "I used to want kids. Sid didn't want them. He never said so but I could tell." He was such a big baby himself he figured she wouldn't pay attention to him anymore. He was probably right. Lilyan could see herself on her kids' raft, drifting out to sea, singing nursery rhymes and a few of the old standards. "I'm glad in a way that I don't have any. I'd be worried sick about rapists and bombs and drugs, muggers, terrorists, school marks."

That was true, Maryann thought; it wasn't the logistics of dentist appointments and Cub Scout meetings, it was the caring that seemed to sap all of her selfness. "You know, it's the first time I've ever been away alone, without either my husband or one or both of my boys except to visit my mother."

"I believe it," Lilyan said. "But cheer up, I'm going to do your nails and make you gorgeous just because. Now smile—aren't you glad you came to New York and found us?"

Maryann didn't deny it. It was all crazy; the Berns were crazy and she hadn't been crazy in a long time. But on the other hand (there always was another hand for Maryann), maybe she found the Berns because she didn't know how to be her own self. Maybe she always needed to be part of someone else's life. She often thought that if Jack and the boys weren't there, she didn't exist. (And if she weren't there with them, they wouldn't exist?) Her own Berkeleian philosophy.

She had called Jack that morning from a pay phone when she went to get milk for Fay. He was paged at breakfast in the dining room.

"Where've you been, sweetheart? I tried you a few times but got no answer. I was getting worried."

"I've been out a lot, darling," she said easily. She considered never telling him about the Berns; he would tease and call them Izzy and Sadie or something like that and manage to spoil it all.

"Are you having a good time?"

"Fabulous."

"That's nice, sweetie," he said, making it sound like a question. He was working very very hard. Everybody was working very very hard.

"That's good, darling," she said. "Have you heard anything from the boys?"

No, everything seemed fine.

Now that was the heart of the call. Guilt. She wasn't missing him, not really (and why not? she wondered), but she had to make sure that he, John and Tommy were all right. Only then could she feel free to do what she wanted to do.

Odd, she thought. When he was away and she was at home, she needed desperately to hear from him. When she was away, obviously, she didn't have the same need. To hear from him. All she felt was relief, pleasure, satisfaction, that they were fine. And there had been no frantic search for a missing Maryann who might be betraying them with absence in a time of great crisis.

Fantasy no. 1: Jack suffers a sudden massive heart attack (a shock to all since he's in perfect health) and they try to reach her at Ginny's apartment. Not only isn't she there but she hasn't advised her beloved family of her whereabouts. Her mother, his parents, her brother, his sister, the hospital, the doctors all try to reach her. Jack is calling her name, unceasingly, in a delirium, the worry and fretting exacerbating his condition.

Fantasy no. 2: Tommy is lost in the woods. Helicopters are searching the dense jungle around the Michigan camp. He is found, finally, weakened by malnutrition in the brief twenty-four hours, and in his semiconscious state calls for her. Mommy, Mommy, I want my mommy. Where is my mommy? (Where is his mommy? Eating bagels and cream cheese.)

Fantasy no. 3: John has been attacked by a maniacal waterfront counselor who has thrust a knife into John's skinny ribs and has left him to bleed to death in an upper bunk and barricaded himself and the wounded boy in the cabin. Police outside issue instructions on a bullhorn; the red lights of the patrol cars skim the night. Where's the mother, God damn it? Maybe his mother could appeal to the killer. These Moms aren't ever around when you need them, the chief of police fumes.

Jack and Maryann send kisses through the phone, promise to tell each other everything, share every detail when he gets back home on Wednesday and she on Tuesday.

"Hey," he says.

"Hey," she replies.

18

At four o'clock Eddie came home to shower and change his clothes. He said they would have dinner on the road, but Lilyan (who had become ravenously hungry) insisted on putting out what she called a small collation, "cold chicken salad and a chilled can of Dr. Pepper's." Or a Bloody Mary, she offered, guzzling hers with hostility since both Maryann and Eddie refused to have one.

Fay wandered into the kitchen for a glass of water and said bitterly to Lilyan, "That a son-in-law of mine should ever marry a girl like you." To Maryann she said, "We're not drinkers, our people. Maybe a highball in company. Your people drink," she said as a fact.

"Ma!"

"What did I say? I didn't say anything bad."

"As you say, a highball in company," Maryann said. See?

They were going straight to Joe's place from Jersey and dressed in preparation for the evening. Lilyan wanted Maryann to wear her fanciest clothes and insisted on giving her a brocade evening bag "to add some class." It was made in India and had a card in it with instructions on how to care for it. "After a few months of its use take a piece of the inner portion of a loaf off your Breakfast (without butter of course) press it all over the Embroidery and it will pick up every bit of dust and is then ready again to glamour with you."

Lilyan glided into the living room in a pale-blue tulle dress, its skirt in layered tiers, her hair swept to a side and cascading down her right shoulder. Maryann wore the

Italian silk suit intended for the Viennese scientist (the British musician?), her blond hair curled and her eyes heavy with green shadow. Lilyan's touch.

"Ma!" Lilyan called. "Don't be mad at me, wish me luck."

But Fay stood in the doorway in a yellow cotton dress and white pumps. Her hair was carefully sprayed with lacquer and her lips shone in shocking pink.

"Who's mad? I'm going with you."

"Are you sure? You haven't been out for a long time, Ma."

"So, it's time I went someplace."

"It's a long ride to Freehold and back," Eddie said.

"You don't want me."

"We do!" Maryann cried.

Eddie hesitated and then gave Fay his arm. "Well, it's another party."

The trip out of the city was uneventful except when they stopped for a red light near Roosevelt Hospital. Two boys were fighting at the entrance, the bigger one banging the smaller boy's head against a post. Lilyan gasped and swept out of the car in a rage.

"Where are you running? They're probably brothers," Fay called to Lilyan, an apparition of tulle flounces bobbing up and down as she strode to the children.

"Stop it this minute," she cried, putting her hand on the older boy's shoulder.

"Don't hit me!"

"I'm not hitting you," she said, backing off, "just stop beating this poor little kid."

The light had changed to green and Eddie was sounding his horn frantically; traffic was beginning to stall behind him.

"He's my brother!" the younger boy said.

"But that doesn't mean he can—"

A woman rushed out the door. "Don't hit him!" she screamed at Lilyan.

"I didn't hit him," Lilyan swore to God. She ran to the car and jumped into the back seat.

"So? Were they brothers?" Fay asked.

Until they got on the New Jersey Turnpike, Lilyan sulked in a corner; Fay, huddled in the other corner, conserved her strength in silence; Maryann brooded about why she didn't miss Jack and who was she if she wasn't John and Tom's mother? But when they passed Newark Airport they started to sing "Someone's in the Kitchen with Dinah" and—this was Fay's request—"The Bells Are Ringing for Me and My Gal." Lilyan was unconcernedly off key, and Fay's voice a harsh quaver; up front, Maryann's natural, soft soprano blended with Eddie's pleasant baritone and Fay, delighted, called them her songbirds.

Maryann saw very little of New Jersey and Eddie told her she didn't miss much.

19

Lou wanted them to wait for him a block away from his ex-wife's house in Freehold. It avoided another argument with her.

He got into the back seat with Lilyan and Fay, exhausted, his skin blotchy.

"You let her beat up on you again?" Lilyan asked.

"Please, Lillie, don't start on me too. I'm getting a nauseous headache." His ex did it to him every time. He liked to call for the children at the house and bring them back, go right up to the front door. None of this sneaking around. But he never escaped his ex-wife's incessant wrath. "So call me up when you've got problems with them, I'm their father, after all, I should know too," he said finally after listening to unremitting complaints. "Call you every time Darlene falls down or we have to decide if Darrell can go on a sleepover? I should chase you all over town on the telephone, in every brothel"—("I don't know any brothels in New York")—"or shacked up with that dancing cow you shlep around? You're not here and we have to make our own decisions. That's reality. That's what I'm teaching your children. Your kids don't have a father." "They do," he cried, "I live, I'm not dead. It was your idea to break up the marriage." "Somebody had to do it."

Etc. etc. etc.

"Are they all right?" Lil asked.

"Who is they? My kids have names. You don't even remember their names."

"I remember," Lilyan said, hurt.

But when Lou leaned back and closed his eyes, Lilyan

moved forward to whisper in Maryann's ear, "Who would call two kids Darlene and Darrell Sheingold?" and tears washed her cheeks. A false eyelash became undone and dipped foolishly over one eye.

They stopped at a McDonald's, where Lou went to the men's room and changed into the tuxedo Lilyan brought along in a garment bag. Eddie suggested they have dinner at a nice place. His treat. A country restaurant. But Fay said certainly not for her, she wouldn't have anything but a cup of coffee and an American cheese sandwich; Lilyan was too ravenous to wait and consumed two Big Macs, a large double order of french fries and a chocolate milk shake.

Everyone stared at Lou, emerging from the men's room in evening clothes. He stepped cautiously around the sticky, prying fingers of a two-year-old in a high chair who reached out, asking "Wot's dot?"

Lou, from within his thin frame, said he couldn't eat anything ("My gorge is full"). He watched Lillie eat, ketchup, mustard, grease, crumbs, smearing her chin.

Eddie was getting irritable. It wasn't the way he had planned the outing.

On the way back to New York they all seemed dulled by Lou's headache and the heat of a late sunset. The New Jersey Turnpike was jammed with cars in a slow march at thirty-five miles an hour. Eddie cursed as he changed lanes minutes before it started to move. Fay dozed. At dusk they passed the Elizabeth oil refineries with the fiery blasts from flare stacks illuminating the eerie gaseous nebula that swarmed over the oil drums and towers, a macabre inferno.

Lilyan began to breathe heavily; she was certain they would be late, and if they got there after ten Joe wouldn't put them on.

At exit 14 Eddie cried "Shit!" so loudly it awakened Fay, who said that one more word like that and she would walk home.

"Anything is better than that fucking mess," he said and got off the turnpike.

At route 1 he found a detour sign and all traffic being rerouted. He was glad to follow a huge Sealtest truck through the maze of back streets.

"Where are we going?" asked Fay, peering out the window.

"I don't know, but the guy up front does."

Cars behind followed Eddie, until they were a crawling electrical snake of reflected lights. Then, suddenly, the truck made another turn and ponderously moved into the parking lot of a Sealtest plant and stopped next to two other ice-cream trucks.

"What—?" Eddie was startled.

The cars behind him streamed into the lot, blocking exits and entrances. Eddie got out of the cab, bellowing, "Go back! Go back!" through the megaphone of his hands.

The cars kept coming and Eddie got up on top of the hood. "I'm lost in a goddamn parking lot! Go back, you fucking lemmings!" he screamed futilely into the braying of horns.

Inside the car Maryann, who had been silent, anxious to avoid the intimate bickering and Lou's headache, began to laugh uncontrollably. Not for years had she laughed with such abandon.

Fay was muttering petulantly; Lilyan began to cry; Lou said "I think I have to vomit" and stumbled out the door.

20

"We could use a drink, Joe."

"I was beginning to give up on you people." Joe was a short, heavyset man in a blue blazer and ascot. He had only recently affected this style to go with the twenty-eight-foot, two-cabin Bertram he bought, which he kept at the Seventy-ninth Street Boat Basin. Lilyan kissed him chastely on the cheek, for Lou's sake. Actually Joe and she used to kid a lot about making it. Joe said it was the most verbose foreplay in the history of sex but when they finally screwed it was not the thrill of a lifetime for either, so they went back to what Joe called "word fucking."

Half the tables were empty; the others were late dinner lingerers, and the supper people hadn't arrived yet. Bobby, the piano player, introduced them with a flourish of chords.

"The new dance sensations, Lil and Lou, straight from Roseland!" He grinned. Joe nervously adjusted his ascot.

When Lil had suggested the dance exhibition he didn't have the heart to turn her down, she seemed so eager. Besides, she might be right. "We'll bring it back. Dinner dancing. Supper dancing. Tea dancing in the afternoon. You'll have a whole new business." Joe wasn't sure he could handle a whole new business.

"How do I look?" Lilyan asked Maryann.

"Beautiful, you look beautiful." Maryann smiled into Lil's tired eyes and hopelessly fluffed the flounces of her dress.

"Pick a song for luck," Lou said to Maryann. "We can dance to anything."

Maryann flushed. She couldn't think. But there was an old song. She and Jack danced to it so many times; it had been revived at Miami U, a favorite. "How about 'You're My Everything'?"

They had a hurried consultation with Bobby. Quickstep, mambo for pace and back to the quickstep tempo.

Lou took two aspirin and swore he was all right and Lilyan gulped the last of a double scotch, while Bobby played and softly sang the refrain:

> You're my everything
> Underneath the sun;
> You're my everything,
> Rolled into one . . .

Then, at his nod, Lilyan and Lou glided onto a small area Joe had cleared of tables, their palms moist, transfixed smiles impaled on their lips.

Applause, applause, applause and some cries for more. Joe was grinning, relieved.

When Lilyan ran to the ladies' room, Maryann followed but the door was locked.

"You were wonderful. Everyone loved it," she called through the door. Lilyan had expected too much of the evening, she thought with a little anger. They were good, the people enjoyed it. What more did she want? "Do you need help?"

"I'm all right." Lilyan's voice was muffled.

Reluctantly, Maryann went back to the table. "She says she's all right," she told them.

They sat, hushed by the distance they had traveled to get to that moment. Lou sipped the rest of Eddie's gin and tonic and Joe sent over another round of drinks.

"It was very nice," he said to Lou, "very, very nice. We'll talk."

When Joe left Lou asked, "You think he means it?"

"He wouldn't say it if he didn't mean it."

"He could have shown a little more enthusiasm."

"C'mon, Lou, you're talking like a kid," Eddie said. "You

were great and the people really liked it. What more do you want?"

"You put your finger on it. Kids. I guess I thought we were Mickey Rooney and Judy Garland. Know what I mean? We put on a show in an old barn, rehearsing in a broken-down shed, no money, and then on opening night suddenly the barn turns into a big razzle-dazzle theater with klieg lights and out of nowhere a cast of hundreds in sequin costumes. And the audience is the whole town, all those poor farmers and working people in black tie and evening gowns." He giggled; his headache was gone and he was getting drunk. He hadn't eaten anything all day.

Lilyan came out of the ladies' room and sat down carefully.

"Well?" Fay asked.

"I think I'm preggers," she said. She was very calm.

Eddie started to make a wisecrack but Lilyan stopped him. "No you don't," she said.

"You're nervous, that's all." Maryann.

"No."

"Maybe you're not figuring right." Fay.

"No."

"You were uptight about tonight. Joe really liked it. He told us." Lou.

"No."

"So you're late from all the excitement. Right?" Lou again.

"Wrong." She leaned over and smoothed his wiry hair.

Married to Sid for years so long ago and no children. God, how she tried. It takes the kick out of sex when you have to screw on schedule, she always said. She remembered how determined she was, counting the days to ovulation, keeping track of the hour, the second. It became a habit to put the thermometer in her mouth as soon as she awakened. If it showed an elevated temperature she would yell—Sid, don't leave yet! For Sid it was a race against his popping off before the toast popped up. The doctors said there was really nothing wrong with either one of them. She went to five different specialists and was pronounced A number one.

When she finally persuaded Sid to go to the doctor it turned out he was okay too. Although his sperm weren't exactly jumping for joy, there was a reasonable amount of activity. But Sid didn't want kids. In fact, soon after their divorce was final he married a friend of Lilyan's: a woman who had had a hysterectomy. (At first Lilyan was hurt, his marrying a friend of hers. She wasn't her best friend, but they were certainly close enough for her to give Lilyan all her leftover Tampax after the operation.)

"You're sure, Lillie?" Fay asked with awe.

"Yeah, Ma, I think I'm sure."

"Maybe it was the hamburger." That was Lou trying one more time.

"Maybe it's a virus, babe," Eddie added.

"Why are you all talking this way?" Maryann cried, "I can't believe what I'm hearing. Why should you *want* it to be a bad hamburger or a virus. *I* hope it's a baby!"

"You don't hope so, do you Lou?" Lilyan asked him sadly. She understood: he had two kids of his own already, he wasn't getting any younger. He was in his let's-wait period. What did he need it for? (What did *she* need it for? It was too late for her. She was too old. She was frightened.)

"Lillie darling," Fay whispered. She expected Eddie's children, but Lil was forty-three.

After a bewildered silence, Lou lifted Lilyan from her chair, and with his arm around her, her head resting on his shoulder, he almost carried her out to the street. She clung to him, feeling helpless, unmoored.

Eddie and Maryann, with Fay between them, found them on the street leaning against a lamppost.

Lou's face looked pinched, wrinkled; he could feel his heart flailing against his rib cage. Diapers. Formulas. Cheesy spit-up. Playgrounds. Again with the sandbox.

"It's a miracle," he said to them quietly. "Lillie always wanted a baby."

"I didn't make up my mind yet!"

Eddie said, "What will you do about your divorce?"

"I'll get the final papers signed. Now there's a reason. Right, Lillie?" Lou's kiss was a delicate touch.

Her face was bloated with tears. "We have to talk about it, we haven't talked yet, I want to go home," she said. She guessed *she* was in a let's-wait period.

"Where did you park, Eddie?" Fay asked feebly.

"Lillie and I are going to my place," Lou said. "She's right. We have a lot to talk about."

"I'll call you tomorrow, Ma."

"Take care." Fear gripped Fay's throat. "You're not a young chickie anymore."

Lil leaned out of the taxi window. "Ma! Is it l'chaim?"

Maryann put Fay to bed. Then she made a pot of coffee and took out of the refrigerator what was left of the chicken salad and chocolate cake. She and Eddie sat for an hour in the kitchen, watching the twelve-o'clock news on television. Once he reached over and, his eyes still on the screen, gently traced the outline of her hand with his finger.

MONDAY

21

Monday morning, with few words of explanation (to herself), Maryann knew it was time to pack her bags. She found it interesting that she didn't maunder; didn't worry about the decision; didn't feel her usual feckless self. She was going to try Ginny's apartment one more time and if the key didn't work she would go to a hotel. She didn't think about going back to Chagrin Falls.

She left a note on the kitchen table for the sleeping, exhausted Fay; she would call her in the afternoon and would see her, she wrote; it wasn't as though she was leaving New York.

Eddie heard her moving around. He didn't seem to require an explanation either. He just said he'd get some clothes on and drive her over there. Maybe he could get the key to turn, he said.

There was a gravid silence between them on the short ride to Seventy-eighth Street, although an undefined urgency pursued Eddie and he felt he had to beat every light.

Up on the top floor at Ginny's apartment door, Eddie inserted the key and with the instincts of a thief tested it deftly with his ear to the lock. Within seconds the door opened and the sun streamed through the trailing plants on the terrace, casting morning shadows in Ginny's flowery, chintzy living room.

It was a surprise to Eddie and Maryann to be there in the sunlight. He closed the door behind them, set aside her luggage, and laid the garment bag carefully on the sofa; then he kissed her. His mouth was full and persuasive and she knew she had been wondering these last two days what his lips would feel like on hers. Wondering all the while his lips formed words. Maryann heaved a huge sigh of relief.

She walked to Ginny's bathroom, reached into her handbag, and located her old diaphragm.

And that's the way it was. The seduction of Maryann Morrison Mansfield was swift.

Maryann could always manage to fantasize an image of a woman whom Jack might take to bed. Did he take other women to bed? She didn't know and she didn't want to know. What you don't know won't hurt you, Agnes, her mother's bridge playing friends told her and each other and the adolescent Maryann couldn't fathom their *knowing,* no less doing. Now at forty, she agreed: if mere suspicion hurt so much, consider the pain of knowing. But that didn't stop the imagery. Someone different from her, she hoped, because then she could convince herself of the logic of simple curiosity for someone opposite to her. For instance: small, petite, raven-black hair, deep brown eyes. That was the woman the tall, blond Maryann confronted in a phantasmal, brilliant dénouement (when she wondered what Jack was doing in Dallas or Detroit).

But (she wasn't finished) the point was she had never conjured up a specific image of her own lover, if she was ever to have one. The classicist, the musician, were vague and undefined; if pressed she couldn't personify them. Was her lover divorced? A bachelor? A widower with small weeping children who filled Maryann with overwhelming guilt because she could not, would not, leave Jack and marry their father, etc., etc.? (Always she entrapped herself with that widower, and her head taking her to a totally different saga.)

Would her lover be an ugly man with an inner beauty or a man so handsome he was ugly, if you get the significance, as Fay would say?

Someone with sensual lips, stocky, curly-haired?

In short, a short Jewish cab driver?

Never.

*   *   *

Eddie had taken off his clothes casually; he felt comfortable in his body covered with black, ringleted hair. He looked at the pale, slim Maryann. (The quintessential shiksa.)

Maryann's frame hummed with nervousness, giving off vibrations of fluttering wings. Eddie quieted her with engulfing arms and the heat of his body. He tried to get her to relax and eventually made her laugh, whispering that they were both like sensitive electronic equipment with buttons ("You have a fascinating clit, Maryann") and knobs and gadgets that had to be stroked, prodded, tuned, he said, urging her to explore his with fingers and mouth (visions of that cool ice-cream cone). Then after a while he suggested that she was like a bialy: soft, yet crusty, tasty, worthy of a big bite, and he tasted her in parts and crevices she never knew she had.

This was Maryann Morrison Mansfield, mother of, wife of, daughter of, sister of, friend of, who might have to seek salvation for eternity as she experienced Eddie's silky circumcised skin. It was different. Certainly different.

No one, least of all herself, expected her to be where she was, her legs spread wide, wet and sticky at their fleshiest part, matting her pubic hair as Eddie, welcomed, slid in again and again, saying that it felt like fighting his way up a sluice. It was a romantic observation.

If Maryann had imagined elegance in her first extramarital encounter, she knew she was doomed as Eddie lunged into her with a final exultant cry.

Maryann was ready for him.

After, he asked (lovingly?), "First time with someone else?"

She nodded.

"Your husband and me?" he asked, some terror growing. "That's it?"

She nodded again, enjoying her answers. Poor Eddie, obviously he felt he had taken advantage of a forty-year-old virgin. He was right, too. She thought she knew everything and now knew she didn't. For instance, Jack was proud of being big and always told her that big was better. She accepted it as fact since he was the first and only man she had known inside her. The discovery was momentous, a virginal truth: medium is good too.

In the bathroom, she looked in the mirror. She hadn't changed. There used to be a college dormitory rumor that you could tell the next morning, just by looking at a girl. All she could see, peering closer, was smeared mascara and glints of light in her eyes, but no strange and mythical metamorphosis. She tried to smile (a good mother is God's sweetest smile from heaven) and ordered out of her head an irrelevant memory of her father telling his cousin's eldest daughter that she wouldn't be able to join the country club if she married the Hebrew fellow she was seeing.

Jack, she thought. Jack, Jack. This is how you do it. (If you do.)

It was a cultural shock.

If she felt sad at all it was because she knew the betrayal was not in the act itself but in using an act of love as amusement, a careless self-indulgence. (A really satisfying game of tennis was less carefree.) Sad because she never knew she had been so available; and more: conscious and aware, fastidiously folding back Ginny's satin bedspread.

"Are you happy?"

"Yes. Yes. Very." So why were huge tears gathering?

Eddie reached her quickly. He had been in the kitchen and found the champagne. "What's wrong? Did I hurt you?" Then, "Wasn't it good for you?" (He groaned: he couldn't believe Eddie Bern was asking was it good for you?)

"No, it was wonderful. I'm very happy, I have a great capacity for happiness," she said, sobbing.

He held her and murmured, "Tolstoy said you can look at a thing tragically and turn it into a misery or take the same thing and use it simply, even humorously. Come on, Maryann, it's not tragic. I won't even mind if you laugh."

That made her laugh. Why were there few regrets, she wondered, and knew that if she was crying it was for the lack of drama. There was no mystery: the butler did it.

She loved Jack and perhaps understood him better at that moment than ever before, though she seemed to be nestling in the arms of a man whom she had met only two days ago. The truth of it was, she didn't know what she was feeling.

The wonder of newness?

The discovery of difference?

The loss of immorality?

He poured champagne into mugs and they sat up in bed, leaning against the headboard. With his free hand he played with her nipples (he had cupped her hand around his balls) and told her everything he knew about girls.

Girls with Big Boobs are Frigid.

Girls with Big Dogs are Frigid.

Flat-chested Girls are Passionate.

If You Don't Remember a Girl's Number You Haven't Laid Her.

If a Girl Kisses You on the Mouth Hard and Then Walks You to the Elevator It Means—

"She wants to make sure you get out of the building," Maryann said.

"You catch on."

Later he did his Jackie Mason routine, the one-liners about husbands, wives, Miami Beach; also his knock-the-mayor patter. It didn't matter which mayor, he'd already driven his cab through the Lindsay, Beame and Koch administrations with the same gags and the passengers always chuckled. He had a ten-block rap, he told her, a twenty-block rap and a thirty-block rap. Beyond that distance he stopped talking.

For the long haul, he liked silence.

22

"You've been here long?" Fay's eyes opened.

"There's a raffle on the corner of Eighty-fourth and Second. The winner gets to sit here and look at you," Eddie said. He had been gazing at her from a chair near her bed.

"Did you know Mimi left? There was a note."

He nodded. "I drove her to her friend's apartment. I got the door open."

"I don't like it. She could be raped in the hallway. A fire could break out." She peered out at him from under a single blue curler. "Marry her."

It was not what he expected. "Ma, you're meshugah. For starters, she's married already."

"A married woman is not always a married woman in this day and age. In my time maybe, but not in your time."

"Believe me, Ma, she has a husband."

"Some husband, sends her to New York alone, a lovely person like that. If he's willing to take chances, his chances are my chances. I bet it's one of those trial separations." She thought a minute and then said, "We'll buy cots. Her two boys can sleep on cots in the living room. We can move the sofa and the big chair to make more room. The sofa will look very nice against the other wall and the chair can go in the corner where—"

"Stop. All the woman did was come to New York for a few days like thousands of other people and you're making up a whole scenario."

Fay held one of his hands. "You got to get married, Eddie. I don't know what will happen to our Lillie, God should be good to her. You think I'm going to live forever? You think this is the way a person should be, without a helpmate? You want a life without children, you and your generation, you and your zero shmopulation? You understand what I'm saying?"

"No," he said, "what's a you?" He hated when she talked this way. "I just came by to see if you're all right. I'll make you a cup of tea."

"I'm alive, I'm alive. I don't want tea." Why does everything have to be a wisecrack with Eddie?

"Ma, don't worry about me, I can't stand it. It makes me feel like a shit." It made him feel like a child who couldn't take care of himself. He should have moved out long ago. Let Lillie worry about Ma.

"All I mean to say," she said now softly, stroking his hand, "is that I will die someday, God forbid, and that lovely person sent to us could be the one who was meant for you. Sure you know her a short time but maybe somewhere up there Lilyan Tashman is looking out for you. What's the saying? The Lord moves in strange ways. Maybe He thought He had to move fast, a hurry-up job."

"You're not even religious," he chided.

"Shhh. Who says I'm not religious?"

"You just want someone to give your hat to."

"She would wear it, believe me. I don't care what you say. In my opinion she is not a happy woman."

Eddie remembered Maryann's tears that morning. He remembered Maryann. It was nuts, ridiculous. Dumb. (Was it possible that maybe his mother was right? Did he want her to be right?)

"I have to go to work. The cab's in a meter." He had better get out of there. "Stay in bed today and I'll see you tonight." He kissed her quickly on the curler.

"Double-lock."

"I always do."

"Eddie!"

"What do you want now?" He was at the front door and walked back halfway.

"I forgot! Lillie won't be here anymore. The little boys can have *her* room." She was triumphant.

23

Maryann didn't remember how she got downtown. She knew she had bought electronic equipment at F.A.O. Schwarz for the boys' train set and she was holding a small package for Jack, a wallet from Dunhill.

Hadn't Jack urged her to shop? She was shopping.

Ohhhh, Jack. Dismay almost brought the sounds to her lips, walking down Fifth Avenue like a woman slightly berserk. By now her conscious self was creating a strong load of guilt, maneuvering and arranging this awkward bundle she assumed she ought to carry. The way she pictured it, it would sit somewhere between her shoulder blades like a knapsack, making her round-shouldered for life.

She made her way into and out of Saks Fifth Avenue without buying anything. It seemed to be a miracle of restraint, but was, in fact, the result of total distraction.

She walked uptown on Fifth Avenue. Maryann wanted to be profound in her thoughts, analytical. She wanted to arrive at wise conclusions a priori, but all she seemed capable of was overwhelming and undefined *feeling*. She knew that wasn't good enough to carry her from here to there, wherever *there* was. Surely a proverb, even an old wives' tale or two, would get her through the next few hours. Pastor Wollsetter would have found appropriate passages in the Good News Bible.

If she remembered correctly, and it was hard to forget, earlier that morning she had tumbled onto her old friend Ginny's bed and had intercourse—that was the word—with a man named Edmund Bern. Edmund Bern, Total Stranger. Edmund Bern a.k.a. Edmund Lowe a.k.a. Eddie Bernstein.

Maryann's eyes darted around wildly. She felt that people

were looking at her. She must be talking out loud to herself.

She passed Doubleday at Fifty-seventh Street and scurried back to it. A bookstore was the right place to think. But no maundering, she warned herself. Real thinking. This was no time to just hope for the best.

She wandered through current fiction, travel, cookbooks, refusing help from the sales people (did she know what she was looking for? they asked), reference books. With wandering fingers she snatched Bartlett's *Familiar Quotations* and, turning pages, found the always reliable Montaigne.

"The thing of which I have most fear is fear." She thought Franklin D. Roosevelt had said that.

"I would let death seize upon me whilst I am setting my cabbages." That meant absolutely nothing to her. But here was a good one.

"If you press me to say why I loved him, I can say no more than it was because he was he and I was I." There was no doubt that was relevant. She did not love Eddie and hoped fervently that he did not love her. (She had gone to bed shamelessly with someone she hoped didn't love her. Gauwgh; with another sound she slid down to the floor to relieve her weak knees.) But certainly what they did was called "making love." So there was an essence of truth. Good old Montaigne.

"He was he and I was I."

I. Who else am I but me, she thought? Where else will I find myself but in me? Not in Jack, not in the boys. Yet what, in fact, really motivated her besides Jack and the boys? There had to be more to her than Jack and the boys. Well, Mrs. Dinosaur, is the core of life sex, even at forty? If so, she got to the core of her life in record time, without a trace of girlish reluctance.

Maryann was oblivious to a woman who stepped over her. Was it true that one's sexual impulse was the ultimate self-ness? The I of me? "Not so, not so," she murmured. There was so much more surrounding that core of self, of that she was certain.

She shifted her position, tucking her legs under her. She

wanted to love and care about Jack and the boys. It was her brightest blessing that they were sharing their lives. But, ah but, what a burden she imposed on them when she required that they be *all* of her life. Her everything. ("You're my everything, everything I need—" She had asked Lil and Lou to dance to it. She must have been carrying around the memory of Jack and her dancing at a mixer at Miami U., dancing to that song, meeting for the first time, about to promise to be each other's everything.)

Why did she want to cry when she felt good? Why did she feel good and want to cry?

A woman and two men stepped back over her knees. It was a narrow passage and Maryann was now sitting on the floor, quite cozily, leaning against a shelf and moving her lips. More Montaigne.

"I find that the best virtue I have has in it some tincture of vice."

Well, let's take that literally, she said to no one, ignoring a man who winked at her. Maryann had been a virtuous woman for forty years. Certainly moral, respectable, whatever that meant, but never mind. The question was, what is vice? Adultery, she presumed. (She was perspiring even in the air-conditioned store.) What about revenge? Was a taste for revenge a vice? Could there have been some element of revenge against Jack? (What you don't know won't hurt you, Jack.)

Maybe she wanted to try adultery even once just to find out that death doesn't occur instantaneously. If she worked at it, she might easily arrive at the conclusion that she— and she was appalled that the word came easily—fucked Eddie for Jack's sake. To be more understanding, more accepting. Just in case she had to know one day the what that would hurt her.

But revenge wasn't the reason. At least it wasn't the basic reason. She didn't fool herself. She had been too ready for Eddie's mouth, his arms, his body. That wasn't an act of revenge that made her groin throb with a rush of blood to the lips inside her thighs. He could have slipped in without a moment's hesitation, not a second's foreplay, that's how ready she had been. (A salesman wanted to know again if she needed any help, getting down on his haunches, chummy, to talk face to face.)

She wanted it to happen, of course she did. Forty going on middle age and Jack her only lover. She might have gone to her death at eighty-five (greedy woman, Maryann) without having known any other man but Jack.

What had once been a point of honor in the past was now a matter of malcontent. She and her friends had dated in the fifties and then married. Some had been Ginnys and some had been Maryanns. The Maryanns were on the cusp, you might say, between the last of a Victorian remnant and the new woman. A pre-pill statistic on a sociological monograph.

Now there was all that open sex in the movies, in books, on panel discussions. People were doing and saying the damnedest things. Nice girls, the heroines, were saying to nice boys, the heroes, on nice shows on television: "I want to go to bed with you."

On *her* television set, in *her* family room, while she, Maryann, was sitting on her sofa munching tacos.

She wanted to be part of whatever was happening before it was too late. At least have a try at it. It, something: she was inarticulate. Maybe she was like the wingless young, migrating to California to quote find themselves unquote. Only she flew to New York instead. Did she think she'd find whatever it was in Eddie Bern's iconoclastic libido?

And had she known she was looking for something? Looking for a crusty bialy.

But what did it mean without love?

(Her right leg was falling asleep and she shifted slightly. That nice salesman leaned down to whisper that he was going on a coffee break and wouldn't she like to have a cup with him.)

Love. Lucky, lucky she wasn't looking for love. She had love in her life. She gave it to Jack and the boys and received love from them. This, this *this* was something else, something new and different.

(It was Jack who had said to her once and sadly: In a short time new is old and different is the same.)

Why was she being so objective? Shouldn't she be frenzied, in torment? Shouldn't she be praying with Pastor Wollsetter on the Doubleday mezzanine floor?

She wasn't.

She thanked the young man politely. Not more than twenty-five years old. Then she smiled a brilliant smile (it was flattering, after all) and said she really had to go home.

She turned east to Madison Avenue and continued to walk uptown. With some conceit she sought glimpses of her buoyant reflection in store windows and was aware that men were looking at her. Not all, but a few. Without turning her head, she knew instinctively which of the men passing by looked back.

At Sixty-eighth Street she bought a scarf for Fay at Halston. It would be an alternate to the ski cap.

Also she barely avoided a disaster at the Hotel Carlyle. A taxi pulled away just as she passed and the passenger in the car turning to look at her was Joe Westcott.

Ten million people in New York. She didn't want to meet Joe Westcott. Remembering what Jack said, she didn't want to hold his hand and certainly not anything else. What are you doing in New York, he'd ask, and how could she tell Joe Westcott what she was really doing in New York?

The cab was halfway up the street but she caught a glimpse of Joe gesticulating wildly as she ran around the corner at Seventy-eighth Street.

(He called the Mansfields weeks later and Maryann said, "I don't believe it! You saw me on Madison Avenue? Oh Joe, what a shame, I didn't notice you at all. I didn't call you because Jack said you were out of town." Lies glistened on her lips.)

She passed Ginny's house, left her packages with the doorman and went on to give Fay the new Halston kerchief.

24

"This is my friend, everybody, remember I told you about her? My best friend from Ohio. Sharon Falls. Well, here she is in the flesh! Ta-raaa!" Lilyan's face was glowing through red-rimmed eyes.

She had been doing a henna rinse and her hands were in rubber gloves covered with muddy brown dye. How do you do? the client said to Maryann, with somewhat of a royal nod, unaware of how ludicrous she looked with a plastic bag on her head. Lil placed the woman under a dryer and led Maryann to a back room, where she poured coffee for them.

"Why did you run off this morning?"

"I've been imposing too much, Lil."

"You're nuts. What are friends for?"

"I didn't exactly run off. In fact, I'm on my way up to visit Fay now. I bought her a Halston scarf. I thought it would be a nice change from her ski hat."

"You're cute," Lilyan said. "If it's a girl, maybe I'll call her Maryann for you and Marion Davies."

"You really ought to go to an obstetrician. You shouldn't guess about something like this."

"I'm not guessing. Lou and I went together this morning. No rabbits, nothing. It's for sure. The doctor said I could do it, I'm healthy like an ox. He knew a lot of women my age who had terrific babies."

"Oh, Lilyan, I'm so happy for you." Maryann hugged her. (All this hugging felt good; she'd go home and hug Aunt Louise.)

"Yeah, it's a fucking miracle, so to speak," she said. "I want to go out and celebrate tonight. If I don't, I'll sit home and scare myself to death. Let's go to Roseland and dance and drink champagne and—" Her face crumbled and she clung to Maryann. "I'm too old! Tell me I'll be all right, tell me I won't die, tell me the baby will be normal! Will you be with me when the time comes? Maybe I'll hate it. I mean being a mother. Maybe I'll be a terrible mother. I don't even know how to be a mother. And I don't want to stay home and make dinner and wait for Lou. I love him, I really do, but I don't want his coming home to be the big event of my day. I want to open my own shop, I always wanted my own shop. I want to da-a-a-nce—" Her mouth distorted in a high ululating cry.

"Listen to me, Lilyan," Maryann said, holding her, patting her, making all the sounds she made with Tommy. "You make it seem like the end of the world, getting married, having a baby. Your baby will be fine. You'll be fine. You'll be a great mother and if you want it, you'll open your own shop too. And you and Lou will dance at Joe's place. People will come from all over to see you. Everybody will be dancing."

Lilyan gazed at Maryann voraciously: her world, her life, being secured by this woman from some crazy place in Ohio, where Lilyan had never been and couldn't remember the name.

"Where's the guarantee? How do you know?"

Maryann thought with some pain that she knew nothing, really nothing. All those happy years didn't mean that she was an expert on anything. "If you want all those things, you'll have them," she said at last. "At least it's possible."

"Do you have everything you want?" Lilyan asked. "I'm not so sure you're all that happy."

"I love my life!" Maryann cried. Who were these people to make her feel that what she had wasn't what she wanted.

"You're shrying," Lilyan said.

"I'm what?"

"Yelling."

"I don't care. Look, Lil, you can call me Mrs. Redbook

all you want but it happens that for me—and now I'm talking about me, not someone else—there was nothing I wanted to do that would have been worth leaving my kids for. Maybe my salary would have bought us a bigger house sooner—well, so what? Having our children, Jack's and mine, that's important, Jack's and mine, and staying home to raise them was not a sacrifice. It was my choice and I'm sick and tired of feeling guilty about it."

"You're shrying again."

"Then I'm shrying! Years ago you were made to feel guilty if you went to work and left your children and today you're made to feel guilty if you don't. I did what I did because I thought it was right and for God's sake, Lilyan, you do what *you* think is best for you and Lou and your child and that will be all right too. There are no rules."

"I hear you," Lilyan said pensively, "I know what you're saying, but don't you ever think about what you'll do when your kids grow up? I can't see you looking out the window like Fay."

That hurt. "I don't look out the window," Maryann said, recalling the kitchen window with the clear view of the road to watch for the school bus and Jack's car. "What will I do? I'll think of something. I'll work at the hospital. I'll think of something."

"I hate hospitals," Lilyan said, shuddering. "That's another part that scares me."

"The maternity ward is the best floor in the hospital. And then there's the baby, like a reward. You *do* want the baby? You have to be sure, Lil. It will be a human being growing up."

"Yeah, don't worry. I want it." She belched. Such heartburn. "A Harvard graduate or a ballerina."

25

"It's me, Maryann."

"Who?" Fay's voice was faint and querulous.

"Mimi."

Fay opened the door and led Maryann to her bedroom where she climbed back into bed, bringing the covers to her chin. She peered balefully at Maryann. The ski cap was on her head; she was prepared to look out the window for Lilyan, Eddie, even Maryann.

"Atlantic City."

"Hm?"

"That's where I went on my honeymoon. Atlantic City. So sit down. Why did you make me worry? A runaway child."

"Fay," Maryann wanted to giggle. She was on the verge of hysteria.

"A beautiful girl like you in a strange city, you should let Eddie take you where you want to go."

"He did," Maryann replied with some irony and hoped she wasn't blushing.

"That's nice." Fay could see the bloom on Maryann's cheeks. A good sign. "Talk to me. Tell me what you did today."

Maryann eliminated the morning from her day, elaborating on shopping at Saks and at the toy store, Dunhill's, browsing in bookstores, she said, and finally, a special surprise, a present for Fay. "You won't guess what I bought you."

"Is it your opinion Lillie should have the baby?" She didn't have the strength to listen to anything. "She's too old to start the whole business. Maybe she shouldn't get married altogether. Maybe she should have the baby and not get married. I never said this to anyone else in my life, God forbid my children should hear me, but I'm not so sure how I feel about marriage. When you stop to think about it, two people living in the same house together, sleeping in the same bed together, making on the same potty year in and year out, maybe it's unnatural. And will this marriage last? With a baby besides? Lillie has bad habits. You want to know why her first husband Sid left her? Because the garbage bag broke. Lillie puts garbage in paper bags, to this day. By the end of the day with the oil, the wet noodles, everything, the bottom gets soaked and then when Sid would take the garbage to the incinerator, the bottom would fall out, all over the floor. The last time it happened, he had his suitcase packed in ten minutes and he was out the door. Does a man leave his wife because the garbage bag broke? I ask you?" Fay shrugged, "Who knows, maybe he does."

While she was talking, Maryann wrapped the kerchief around Fay's head, tying it back behind her hair. "Stunning," Maryann said, "look at yourself in the mirror. One of the beautiful people on the Riviera."

"Let me see." Fay smiled at herself archly. "You're some wonderful girl, Mimi darling," she said, cheered. She should cut out her tongue talking about marriage that way with Mimi when what she wanted was, well time will tell. "Come, just for that I'll tell your fortune. Give me my cards." She shuffled them expertly and found the queen of hearts. "That's you, darling," Fay murmured. She placed it in the center and then dealt the cards, spreading them on the blanket face up until they formed a spoke-and-wheel effect. She kept muttering comments as though they were incantations. "The hearts are love, the diamonds are money." Oy, there was the ace of spades, but it was in an unimportant position. God was good. The ace of spades was big trouble. Terrible trouble. She never told young girls how much trouble. If the card showed up where it shouldn't, Fay always said, "Eh, a little aggravation."

Intermittently, Fay would put a card face down on top of the queen of hearts until there were five. When all the cards were dealt, she lifted the five cards in the center and spread them out in her hand with a smile of expectation.

No Eddie. The king of spades was not in her hand. So where was he when she needed him? Finally, she found some kind of pattern. "Changes," she said. "There will be big changes in your life." Well, that was something. "See, here is the ten of diamonds and the eight of clubs. I can't tell you what kind, but Important Changes. Maybe you have an idea of what I refer to?" Fay was being sly.

"Well," Maryann grinned, "maybe. I've been doing a lot of thinking the last couple of days."

Fay hummed with satisfaction. "Let's do it one more time." She shuffled the cards again and spread them out as before. This time the jack of hearts was among the five cards that covered the queen. The jack of hearts, like the other night. Whoever he was, he wasn't Eddie. Fay pushed the cards aside; they angered her. "What do they know?" she muttered.

Maryann straightened the covers. "Tell me what it was like growing up in New York."

Fay plucked at Maryann's skirt, like a child. "Eddie is a beautiful person."

Maryann sat down on the chair weakly. Had Eddie dared to tell Fay about their morning?

"Some people think writers are bums, but mark my words, someday he'll make it big in the writing business and if not he'll own a fleet of cabs. We always thought he would be a dentist because his uncle Moses said he was going to put him through dental school. But Moses had terrible teeth, and by the time Eddie was in college, Moses was wearing dentures and lost all interest in Eddie's dental career. But it didn't matter"—her voice wavered—"because my Eddie didn't want to be a dentist anyway. Clumsy fingers. He always had dropsy. Mimi."

"What?"

"My Eddie always had a lot of girl friends you know. He could have anybody."

"I'm sure. He's very"—what was Eddie?—"charming."

"Ah, you noticed his charm, God bless him."

"Oh, yes," Maryann held Fay's hand, "I noticed his charm."

Fay shifted in the bed and groaned. "I read somewhere once that an old person is like a bird perched on a tree. The tree is the tree of life. You get the significance? As the person gets older, the bird goes higher and higher, the better to fly away. The birds on the lower branches don't see too much because the leaves are thick on the branches lower to the ground. But as the bird moves up the view becomes clearer and the bird can see on all sides. Far away, below, above. And what I see up there, that you can't see down there, is that it's your health that counts and so long as the children are well."

"I'm afraid I'm sitting on a branch in the middle of the tree."

"Well, it's still full of leaves where you are and you can't see nothing," she said.

Her Eddie should be all right. Lilyan should come through with flying colors. What a dopey expression, flying colors.

26

"You want to know a secret?"

It was seven o'clock in the evening and Maryann and Eddie were sitting on Ginny's terrace, drinking beer from cans and eating triple-decker sandwiches Eddie brought from the Madison Avenue delicatessen. Turkey, tongue, swiss cheese, cole slaw and Russian dressing.

"What?" Maryann's mouth was full, the food exotic.

"I'm really not a smartass. Seriously, I wisecrack for the types I know, they expect it of me. Who knows, maybe I'm drawn to women who can't deal with more than a stand-up comic. But you're different. You're a mensch. A real menschy type." Russian dressing on his chin. Maryann reached over and wiped it off.

"The other day I asked you something," she said. "But that was before— Anyway, I'll ask you again. Are you going to drive a cab and go from woman to woman forever? Is that going to be your life?"

"What the hell are you talking about? You know I'm a writer." He chewed furiously. Either the sandwich or his thoughts were causing a knot in his solar plexus. "A lot of writers were old before they made it; Kafka was even dead. Don't worry about me. Someday you'll read the reviews that say I'm a writer of such intellectual genius and yet so touching and funny one laughs and cries simultaneously. The accolades will be printed in ads in the book-review sections all over the country, two-liners from famous writers, with little asterisks next to each. I'm so sure of it I'll tell you something that will really show you how sure I am. Or crazy. Crazy Eddie. You know, reporters don't always quote you accurately and sometimes, when I can't sleep at night, I compose interviews with me in my head, and I worry that some jerk will quote me wrong and people will think me unintelligent, worse, a shmuck. I'm already worried about interviews. That's how certain I am that I'm a writer who will write. You laugh," he said, when she laughed. "Remember that I told you."

He lifted her to her feet and with elaborate care wiped his mouth and then, tenderly, wiped hers before kissing her on her lips, her eyes, her throat.

"There's a shiksa in Chagrin Falls," he sang off key.

His body was so warm and hard, holding her. She felt his strength, and just once more, it won't matter. It's not like it's the first time, Maryann was thinking when the phone rang.

"Maybe it's someone for Ginny," she said. The phone startled her; she assumed they were alone in New York.

"Forget it," he murmured, holding her close, rocking her as though in a dance.

Maybe it was Jack to tell her something about the boys. Maybe it was Jack to ask, Hey, are you having a fabulous time?

"Hello?"

"Maryann, oh, God, Maryann!" It was Lilyan, crying, choked. "Fay is dead!" she screamed. "Where's Eddie? Do you know where Eddie is?"

Maryann in silence held out the receiver to Eddie. The color of sex had vanished from her cheeks.

"It's Ma! She's dead! I got home and she's sitting in a chair in the kitchen, dead! Like she just slipped away from us."

"Is Lou with you? Call him right away! I'll be right over, Lillie, Lillie, sh, sh."

He turned to Maryann, awe supplanting grief. "I just saw her around twelve o'clock, I wanted to make her a cup of tea. Can you believe it?"

Maryann kept shaking her head, terrified. No, no, she couldn't believe it.

"I guess we're orphans now, Lillie and me."

Always a wisecrack, he thought bitterly.

27

(Fay perched awhile at the window, her new kerchief a colorful plume. It was too early to expect someone, anyone. Lillie, Eddie; she couldn't recall whether Maryann said she would return. Habit drove her. It was the thing she did, looking out the window for them. Although she knew that if she started to look too soon, she would become anxious and worried even before she could reasonably expect anyone home. The anxiety churned in her stomach. Sometimes she thought that she didn't feel like herself unless she had this *noodjy* feeling.

She had risen from her bed mostly because she started to think about Abe. Her husband. He should rest in peace. She hadn't given him his name for some time. Only to Abe had she said Abe. Your father, she called him to the children. My husband to friends, and Mr. Bern to strangers. She thought of them locked fiercely in each other's arms, Abe and Fanny—he refused to accept her personal image of Fay Wray—in a concert of heavy, panting breathing. Abe sweating. From the very beginning they clung to each other, the better to destroy each other. Love was a struggle to the end. Why was she thinking about such things now, so many years later? It wasn't as if she *wanted* to think about it. It must be because she tried to remember her honeymoon in Atlantic City and one thing led to another.

Like in the morning he would cough and spit up phlegm, almost a retching—he was a heavy smoker—and spit into the kitchen sink. And how he would come home from work with a shmaltz herring from the pushcarts, wrapped in old newspaper. He would spread out the paper on the kitchen table, sometimes it was the *Mirror*, sometimes the *Journal-Amer-*

ican, and read a little bit through the grease stains while scaling the fish with a small knife. Then he would cut off a piece and chew, his strong teeth grinding the salty flesh. In that way he was a sensual man, Abe.

And she? She wanted to dance—that's where Lillie got her talent—and be Fay Wray. The evening is young, she used to say, although Abe was finished for the night. Irene Dunne had said it in one of her pictures, she forgot which one. The evening is young, she remembered saying to Abe time and time again. But what did he know about evenings; that the evening was a more beautiful beginning than the start of the day. She was always a night person, to this day. Abe ate his dinner, listened to the radio a little bit—he liked the comedians, Ed Wynn, Joe Penner, and when television started he never missed Milton Berle—and then he took her to bed with the same appetite with which he ate the herring. He would fall asleep easily; he was a hardworking man. That much she gave him. He worked with the barrels down at Katz's and always smelled of pickles and brine.

It was a noise in the kitchen that startled her. Had one of the children come in and, dreaming crazy things, she missed the pleasure of seeing a familiar, beloved figure walking down the street?

"Eddie, is that you? Lillie?" Hm. "Mimi?"

When she walked into the kitchen she saw the young boy. Not older than sixteen. He had just stepped through the window from the fire escape. His face glazed by summer heat and fear at finding someone at home.

"Oy vey," Fay said, clutching her chest, her sudden, tumultuous pulse sealing off her breath.

"Lady—" The boy seemed to hover, suspended: to go back through the window or take a step nearer? though he didn't know exactly what he would do if he should come close enough to the old woman.

"Stay away from me," she wheezed, her lips numb. They glared at each other and then—perhaps it was the incipient frail fuzz on his upper lip—Fay's fury consumed her fear.

"Not another step," she warned, shaking her finger. "To me you do this? In my house? I'm not even outside with all the nuts? Do you get the significance? To me, Fanny Bernstein, you climb into *my* kitchen in broad daylight, the sun is still out? Get out of my house before I call the cops!" A scream started deep in her throat.

With the eyes of a supplicant—before this he had accosted people only on the streets, where he could run—the boy moved quickly toward her. He had to shut her up. And it was then that Fay stepped back in simple fright and fell into a chair behind her. Sitting upright and before the boy's eyes, Fay made mewling sounds before she died, untouched and unscathed.

"Shit, motherfucker, shit, aw shit," the boy wept. Although her eyes were open, he knew she was dead. Her head lolled and her body seemed emptied.

He hadn't laid a finger on her. It wasn't his fault. Wake up, lady! Wake up!

He wasn't even aware that he was whimpering as he wandered aimlessly around the room. Should he go back through the window? He would have to climb over both back-yard fences again. His mind was muddled; the body of the old lady terrorized him. He saw the portable television set on the kitchen table, the blender, the radio. Something. Nothing. Motherfucker. He grabbed an empty carton from under the sink, a cockroach crawled out, and he fled through the front door. If anyone saw him on the stairs he would be a delivery boy from a supermarket with an empty carton. Clean, he was clean. Oh, Christ. See? He had nothin' on him.

TUESDAY

28

In the kitchen Lou and Lilyan were dancing, moving sadly to the dim sounds of music from the radio. Lou had one arm around her and with the other he rubbed her belly. Her head rested on his shoulder and her arms, uncaring, hung at her sides. She was crying softly. For Fay, for the wonder that Lou was such a tender man.

They had called distant cousins, neighbors, friends, a sister-in-law in Florida. The funeral would take place the following morning at eleven o'clock. Fay belonged to a burial society and Abe waited for her in Mount Hebron Cemetery in Queens. Side by side they would lie with a double stone their headboard. Unwillingly Maryann remembered Fay's complaint about marriage. The same house, the same bed, the same potty . . . Poor Fay. Maryann almost smiled. But she must have wanted it this way or she wouldn't have prepared a place for herself alongside Abe.

They talked about how they had just been with her. Eddie to make her a cup of tea. (He might have aggravated her condition with his intransigence, but he refused to believe it.) Lilyan called after seeing the doctor and had a long talk with her; even Lou got on the phone to say a few words. (Maybe the shock of knowing she would be a grandmother finally and her fears for Lilyan's life caused the attack, but that couldn't be.) And Maryann said, "I just saw her this afternoon and brought her the scarf. She told my fortune." (Maybe her staying with them was too much excitement, but no, Fay seemed to enjoy it.)

"The scarf was the last gift she ever received. Do you mind if I keep it? I know my mother appreciated it," Lilyan said.

So what happened?

"Nothing happened that shouldn't have happened," Eddie said. "She's been sick for years. She had a lousy heart and high blood pressure. She died and that's life."

"You think so?" Lilyan whispered to Lou. That can't be life, she thought, before falling asleep in his arms.

It was decided that Maryann would go home as planned that afternoon. She knew it was time to leave. Her being there was now an aftermath; the episode was over and, she felt, her presence almost an intrusion.

She had helped by shopping for the meal to be served when the friends and family came back after the funeral. Hard-boiled eggs, they told her, some lox, sturgeon, coffee cake, cold cuts. Ham?

"Not ham," Lilyan said. "I know we eat everything, but not tomorrow." Go explain.

Eddie told her quantity was important. "People seem to have a need to sustain their own lives on the occasion of someone else's death." He hated the people tomorrow would bring.

Lou led Lilyan to her bedroom and Eddie and Maryann sat across from each other at the kitchen table as they had sat on Sunday night.

"In the end nothing matters, Maryann," he said after a while. "Don't tell your children, though."

"I won't," she said sadly.

"She said sadly." He smiled. Nothing mattered. Some message from a man of such promise as he. Is. Was. Once. Fuck.

"What will you do?"

"When I grow up?" He watched her twisting a paper napkin and wondered how he would remember her, if at all. What would he tell himself? And there was a girl from Chagrin Falls I could have married but.

They were silent, presumably thinking about Fay. In fact, they had nothing to say to each other.

29

Maryann boarded the plane. It would be a short ride, barely time for the snack they served, and she had a lot to think about. The four days that had passed were four weeks, four months, four years. New York was below on a rare clear day, the hard-edge outline concealing sentient lives.

She contemplated the circle of her days in which she moved in a rich roundness, always coming home. She thought of those things she wouldn't speak of to Jack and what Jack would say to her. (I love you, Maryann, and of course he did.)

A lot to think about, but what was the rush? There was no tally, no list she had to check off before the end of the flight. Or the end of her life, for that matter.

A list of things to do. A timetable of her days that told her where Jack was. Tom? John? But Tommy and John were en route into the world where it was important for *them* to know where they were. And Jack was already there. Now it was important that she know where *she* was.

A new kind of vitalizing apprehension traveled from her brain to her stomach, where she experienced most of the sensations that told her something was about to happen. Something new (could she deal with new?) beyond the beloved commitment and loyalty to those oh, most dear people who waited for her in Chagrin Falls. (With an effort she willed herself to deny the old fears that without her attention they would die.)

Of one thing she was certain, however. There were no regrets. She wasn't sorry she was a mother and a wife. There was no way for it to have been otherwise; no possible way to have acquired, twenty years ago, the distant consciousness of today's generations with their own particulars of life and future. She had done what she wanted to do in her own time and place.

Now she was alive, she was alive, and ready to move on. (And should she feel guilty about not having marched, signed, joined all those women who made her present possible?) Yes. She was beholden to them. They had known something she didn't know.

But in exchange for guilt she would give them a gift. Something *she* knew that *they* didn't know. Well, whom could she tell? It was hardly a popular notion yet, and who would be receptive enough to listen? (Maryann glanced at the young woman sitting next to her, sipping a ginger ale. Perhaps she would start with her.)

Listen: Yes. Whatever you want to be, be. But—and this is what she had to say—it is foolhardy to deny the need for someone else in one's life. Need. Not dependence, but need. An old instinct of the heart, a vital extension of the expression of oneself.

Everything is possible, young woman slurping the empty container, poking the ice cubes with a straw, but please don't forget that they're still writing love songs.

(Maryann is in the lobby of the Beverly Wilshire Hotel and there is Lou, taller than she remembered him, his age apparent in the fullness of his face.

He calls, Mimi? although he is certain it's she. They are genuinely pleased to see each other.

He says he is with his son, who is checking out the candy counter, and Maryann tells him she is meeting her husband in San Francisco to visit their older son at Stanford. Lou says, You go to Stanford and I go to Disneyland. Ha ha. He had to be in L.A. on some real-estate deal so he decided to take the boy since it's spring vacation at kindergarten.

Lil is great, he says. They bought a building on East Eighty-fourth Street with a storefront and turned it into a large beauty salon, very successful. They live on two floors above the shop and rent out the rest. Renovated the whole thing, Maryann ought to come and bring her family. He sold his business—look, no rash—and got involved in real estate. And you? he wants to know.

Tell Lil that I was in Los Angeles for a conference of hospital administrators. She'll get a kick out of it.

He says they appreciated her calling when the baby was born and she says that she knew when it was expected and took a chance. He tells her that the blanket she sent was the kid's best friend. There's still a piece of it he won't part with. But not even an address so they can say thank you. Shame. And no, they gave up the Joe Beamish thing. No time, Lillie is busy day and night; but they manage to go to Roseland at least once a week.

And Eddie, she asks finally. Lou doesn't let on he knows there was something going on between Maryann and Eddie.

Lillie told him although he doesn't know how she knew.

He says that Eddie is Eddie. He has an apartment on the top floor of their building and he's still driving a cab and going out with girls. He types a page here and there; it's the longest and oldest novel ever written. Now Eddie claims it's about a survivor searching in the rubble for love. He keeps kidding about going to Vestspitsbergen to find a wife. It's in the Arctic. Lou shrugs his shoulders, raises his eyebrows, puts his entire body into the wordless message: What can you do?

Maryann has to go; Lou has to go. He calls over a five-year-old boy. He is chunky, rosy, and wears a Mickey Mouse hat. He resembles Lilyan.

This is Freddy, Lou tells Maryann. We named him for Fay, but it's really for Fredric March.)